Tell me the Secret

Marie Rowan

Published in 2017 by
Moira Brown
Broughty Ferry
Dundee. DD5 2HZ
www.publishkindlebooks4u.co.uk

Tell me the Secret was first published
as a kindle book in 2015.

Copyright © Marie Rowan

The right of Marie Rowan to be identified as the Author of this work has been asserted in accordance with the Copyrights, Designs and Patents Act 1988.

All rights reserved. No part of this book may be reprinted or reproduced or utilised in any form or by any electronic, mechanical or other means, now known or hereafter invented, including photocopying or recording, or any information storage or retrieval system, without the permission in writing from the Publisher.

ISBN 978-1-5220-4132-0

About the author

Glaswegian Marie Rowan has had several books published, both fiction and non-fiction. Her biography *Dan Doyle: The Life and Death of a Wild Rover* about Scotland's first bad-boy football superstar became a best-seller. She has a wicked sense of humour which is most evident in her grisly novels, *Once Upon a Murder* and *Death is Murder.* Marie's time spent holidaying and writing on the islands of Mull and Iona inspired her to write *Don't Go There!* and *Tell me the Secret.*

Marie spent her working life as a school teacher in Glasgow.

Dedication

For Chrissie Duncan, Salen, Isle of Mull, and Abby MacKenzie, Dervaig, who led me on a truly magical tour of the Ross of Mull to discover the mysterious Mariota stone.

Acknowledgment

This book was written at the suggestion of my friend Alan Jack, Salen, Isle of Mull. I am also deeply indebted to Alan for permission to use his hauntingly atmospheric photograph of the sacristy door of Iona Abbey for the cover of this book.

Tell me the Secret

chapter 1

Frenzied lightning ripped across the darkened sky. Muirne cowered deeper into the yellow gorse and waited for the ear-splitting racket of thunder. Within seconds, it exploded violently and the ground seemed to tremble beneath her. She felt the gorse sting her arms and its fallen razor-sharp needles pierce her feet through her soft, leather shoes. She waited there until the frightening battle in the skies above was over. The lightning and thunder raged relentlessly at each other. Muirne held the precious parcel close to her body to keep it dry. Her father's mid-day meal. Bread, cheese and ale. The bushes were so dense they gave her shelter from the sudden heavy downpour that followed, soaking everything around. Muirne stayed within the protection of the gorse until she saw the yellow sun sweep quickly over the land once more and she could hear again the voices of the villagers down by Loch Assapol. She looked down to the loch's edge then away to the water that flowed by the little church below. She smiled as her friends raced along the stream to their favourite fishing spots.
"Are you coming?" they shouted .
"Later!" she called back. Maybe she would join them as soon as she had given her father his mid-day meal. Stone-masons worked hard and her father was one of the best. Muirne smiled to herself with pride. He did carvings for the

abbot of the great abbey of Iona. She loved the way all the others admired the designs he cut into the walls and cloister pillars, the stories he told with his carvings. He was a great artist. Birds, animals, he made them all come to life in stone and the designs in their own little church of St Ernan's were like intricate puzzles as the trails ran above and under each other. Muirne shook the gorse needles from her long, red-gold hair. She looked back and waved to some more of her friends on the path above the field as they made their way to Scoor beach to collect seaweed from the shore. The rays of the sun had coasted lazily across the sky but were now disappearing behind silver-edged, black clouds that seemed to have come out of nowhere and darkness came hurtling across the land.

The blue clumps of lavender caught her eye as she picked her way carefully down the sloping field and along the edge of the stream. She was tempted to wade across but it was still running fast from the heavy rains of the previous week. She clambered back up onto the sloping high bank. Ahead lay the small, wooden bridge that crossed it as part of the well-trodden pathway leading to St Ernan's church. She looked up and saw her father by the far gable of the building.
"Father! Your bread and cheese!" she called down to him and she shielded her eyes from the sun as it came out once more. He didn't seem to hear her. She sighed and waved to get his attention. Muirne now saw that he was speaking to one of the monks from the great abbey on Iona who came over the waters of the Sound of Iona to the church to take the services. Maybe she should wait where she was till the monk left. She could then cross the bridge and catch her

Tell me the Secret

father before he began working again. Muirne looked back up the hill. The others had become small specks on the landscape as they head for Scoor beach. She turned and looked down across the stream and frowned.

"Father!" she called again only much louder this time for her father had begun to move away with the black-hooded monk whose face was hidden by the hood of his robe. She ran across the bridge as by now they seemed to be heading quickly for the loch. She could see one of the abbey's boats beached there by the edge of its sparkling waters. "Drat!" The monk had probably brought a small stone in his boat for her father to repair. She knew that her father was not due to be going there for several weeks. It must have special significance for the abbot himself perhaps. If it was such business, her father would not like to be interrupted. He relied on the money they paid him to feed all of them and since her mother had just vanished almost a month ago, her father had enough worries without Miurne annoying the monks.

She sat down on a rocky outcrop by the church door and waited for him to return. His tools lay close-by where he had been working. The blue clumps of lavender were stirred by the slight breeze and Muirne gave into temptation. Her grandmother could definitely use them for she had not slept since Muirne's mother had gone. She would be back in a short time. If she put the food on the window ledge of the church building, it would be quite safe from passing animals and she would still be able to keep an eye on it.

The clumps of lavender and rosemary were plentiful and more time had passed as she picked them than Muirne had realised. Father would have spotted the food parcel for

Tell me the Secret

it was wrapped as usual in a small hemp sack with purple stripes her grandmother had smeared on it with the dye from heather. She looked as soon as she came within sight of the window. It was still there. Father had not come back. Muirne reached up and lifted it down. She could hear voices coming nearer and walked to the far corner of the church. She was pleased to see the other villagers returning with their days catch. She was sure Father would have told them how long he would be gone for he knew that Muirne would come to the church with his meal and ale. They would pass on the message for him. She hoped it would be soon for then she would be able to hurry back home and give Grandmother her herbs while they were still fresh.

"Waiting for your father, Muirne?" Alasdair was the best fisherman in their village.

"Yes. I've got his meal here. Did the monk want help lifting a stone from his boat?" asked Muirne as the villagers passed by slowly hauling nets to be mended outside their cottages. Alasdair's wife kept a firm hold on the tiny child beside her as she answered.

"What monk?"

"The one who came to see Father. His boat was beached beside yours." The woman laughed a pleasant sound before speaking.

"Too much playing in the sun, Muirne. Your father's been working here at the church all morning. He came down to chat when we first came."

"Not early this morning, just a short time ago. Just as you waved to me."

"We haven't seen him since early on, have we, Alasdair?" Her husband shook his head.

Tell me the Secret

"Certainly not lately."

"And ours are the only boats on the loch today so far," said another villager, frowning.

"But he left here as I came down the hill and walked with a monk towards the boat. Look, his tools are here."

"No-one beached a boat on the lochside, we haven't seen any monk, mysterious or otherwise today and so it looks like your father has walked off into Tir Tairngiri, the Land of Promise." Everyone laughed and moved on. "He'll turn up. The loch can be dazzling in weird weather like this, throws up shadows and the like, Muirne."

"I definitely saw the two of them do just as I've told you," Muirne insisted to the fisherman and his wife. The woman took Muirne's arm as her husband joined the others.

"Now, Muirne, your grandmother has the second sight. Wise-women. Runs in your family. Generations of the women have had it. Come home and speak to her."

"No. Will you give her these herbs? I know my father's gone over the water to Iona and I'm going there right now to find him."

chapter 2

Muirne waved as the driver of the cart turned off the road leading to the ferry point directly opposite Iona. She had been lucky. If he had not stopped to talk to a friend, she would never have got here so quickly. It was a good few miles to walk. It was just about mid-day and the small isle across the mile-wide water lay sleepily in the spring sunshine, its squat abbey tower lording it over the church and outbuildings. Suddenly Muirne stopped dreaming and raced down to the wooden platform. The boat was getting ready to leave.
"Wait! Wait for me!" she shouted breathlessly and scrambled on board before anyone could stop her. She sat looking prim and proper amongst the frowning nuns and scathing looks of the monks. Suddenly she felt a slight tap on her arm.
"Yours, I believe." Muirne nodded to the nun and stuffed the piece of cheese wrapped in coarse cloth back into her hemp sack. No-one spoke as they were rowed across the water. Better still, no-one asked her for her fare for Muirne did not have a single coin on her and the offer of a piece of the cheese that had fallen into the bottom of the boat was likely to be refused.

Muirne leapt out of the boat as it was beached on the sand and ran along the cobbled street towards the abbey.

Tell me the Secret

She knew her father had been helping to carve figures on the pillars of the cloisters recently. That's where he would be. She would surely find him there . Clasping her small parcel firmly under her arm, she tried to look as invisible as possible for she knew the monks were not keen on children playing near their church. Except there were no children on the island just then, only the monks in the abbey and the nuns a short distance away in their nunnery.

A short time later, Muirne stood alone in the silence and wondered what she should do. No-one had seen her father that day. He was not even expected there for another week as he was finishing work at St Ernan's. No he wasn't, Muirne had wanted to shout but hadn't. The green grassy patch of the cloister garden, enclosed by the four, pillared walkways, was lush after the early spring rains. She sat down in the shade, her back against the cool, stone and wondered what she should do next. She felt hungry and her father would not mind if she ate some of his cheese and maybe a bit of his bannock while she thought about what she should do next. Suddenly she woke up with a start.

"What?" said Muirne confused for she must have fallen asleep. A boy's voice had shattered her dreams.

"I said a mouse has just made off with a piece of your cheese." A pleasant enough voice but he was now laughing at her.

"You mean you ate it!" she said accusingly.

"I do not!" he answered indignantly. Muirne gazed after the boy as he stormed away and left her alone once more. What strange clothes he was wearing. Her quick temper again. Anyway, her business was not his business. She looked at what was left of the cheese. Nibbling signs right enough.

Tell me the Secret

A feeling of guilt caused a deep blush to cascade over her freckled face. I'll bet the mouse just beat him to it, she said to herself as she brushed the crumbs from her brown woollen tunic. She stood up and swallowed the piece of the bannock that had been in her hand. Where was Father? Who was that boy? He could not be in the abbey learning to be a monk because he would have been wearing a black habit. A visitor? Possibly, maybe even a king's son for her father said kings had once often visited the island. But Muirne did not remember seeing him pass through their village and anyone bound for Iona had to pass that way. Unless he had come by sea. Maybe from Islay which lay to the south. That would be it. She spotted a small drinking well at the far end of the cloistered walk and drank deeply from it. But a third small handful stopped in mid-air as an odd sighing sound came to her and made her breathing almost stop. A woman's sad, pleading voice. Tell me the secret? it seemed to breathe. But where was it coming from? And what secret? Muirne listened intently and a cold hand seemed to take hold of her very heart as she recognised the voice. Her mother's. But where was she?

"Mother!" cried Muirne, "Mother, I'm here. Where are you?" But her own voice just echoed endlessly round the pillared garden then total silence. Muirne was shaking. Was she still dreaming? But her brain was totally alert and it told her she had not been mistaken. Then the sound came again, seeking and searching endlessly, it seemed, along the walkway, round the pillars, wrapping and enfolding its sad, desperate plea round Muirne till she clasped her hands over her ears to blot it out.

Tell me the Secret

"Tell me the secret," it had begged sobbing over and over again till Muirne could stand it no longer. But now she knew where it was coming from. Inside the church itself.

Muirne ran along the covered passageway and burst into the dim church, pushing aside the heavy wooden door as if it were made of straw. But the sighing sound had now stopped. She was alone in the long, silent nave that led finally to the altar. The stone-flagged floor felt icy cold through her soft leather shoes. The deep silence was eerie and she felt slightly nervous and vulnerable. What should she do? Suddenly an odd fluttering sound came from further down the nave. From somewhere off to her left came a sound she could not quite place. It was different to what had so frightened her some minutes before and yet somehow seemed to be drawing her to it against her will. She moved slowly towards it, being led on by some unseen force. The noise grew louder and louder until the sound of birds in distress made her rush to the sacristy door. A tiny room off the nave, it was a forbidden place, she knew that much from her father, allowed only to monks of the abbey. The wooden door was open just a little. Muirne pushed it slightly and in the darkness within, saw only what was lit by a solitary flickering candle placed on the narrow ledge of a small, pointed window. All around, fluttering wildly were dozens of small, captive birds in total panic. As Muirne threw the door further open to release them, they rose up in a cloud of beating wings and each, as it flew through the open door, became a dark blur and then a soaring black raven. Muirne pressed herself flat against the cold, sandstone wall and watched as they massed as one black, shifting body and then, with beating wings, escaped joyously from their prison through the door Muirne had left half-open for them and into the freedom of the air and then the sky outdoors. The silence they left behind lasted only a fleeting moment. Her eyes were drawn to a beautiful, golden chalice placed on a small table by the faint, sweet chirping of a bluebird. Its tiny head only just managed to peep out over the rim from inside. Muirne hurried over to help.

"Leave it!" Muirne turned slowly and the realised a figure was sitting at a sloping, high desk in a corner of the dimly lit room behind the door.

"But it's hurt," she said.

"I said you are to leave it alone." Muirne had the horrible feeling this might be the mysterious monk she had seen with her father. A sudden thought rushed through her mind. "Tell me the secret!" she blurted out. Why had she said that? Where had that thought come from? Her hand stroked the little bird as it sat in the chalice. The monk ignored her question.

"The bird is injured. I'm taking care of it." The monk seemed completely unaware of the incredible transformation of the other birds. He had spoken as if nothing unusual had happened. He continued writing in his huge book. Not once did he look across at Muirne, not once did she see his face so deep was it hidden in the shadow of his hood. Muirne swallowed hard and decided to try again.

"Tell me the secret." The bird chirped sweetly. The monk dipped his quill in the black ink and ignored her. "Well, tell me where my father is."

"I know nothing of your father." He kept on writing.

Tell me the Secret

"Where is my mother? I heard her voice in the cloister. I would like to see her. She was asking to know the answer to some secret. Tell me what it is. Please tell me."

"I don't know what it is," the monk said softly. His hand had stopped writing as he spoke and he seemed to have come to some sort of decision. She still could not see his face. "Yes, there is a secret, but what it is, nobody knows. I can only tell you one thing concerning it for I know nothing else. That demand when it is answered will bring your mother back to you." Muirne could hardly believe what she was hearing. They all thought that her mother was lost to them forever. They thought that she had somehow drowned in Loch na Lathaich beside her village. Her heartbeat was racing as she spoke.

"So who has the answer? Where can I find them and discover it?" The monk sighed deeply before answering.

"It's not that simple." He sat back and the dim light from the candle by the small window fell upon the page of the book he was writing in and revealed the stunning colours of his decoration. He examined it critically for a moment and then seemed to remember Muirne was still in the room. "The answer to 'Tell me the secret' is in four parts and has to be completed before sunset. Should you accept the challenge and enter the other world, if you fail to complete the entire task, you will not be able to return and will be condemned to roam those lands forever. That's all I know. Now, the bird will be fine. It has injured a wing but it's healing. Now go, I can't help you anymore." He dipped his quill in the ink yet again and Muirne knew she would find no more answers in that room.

Muirne walked slowly and thoughtfully back into the church again then stopped. She looked back and the sacristy door was now firmly closed against the world. She shivered and walked back outside into the warmth of a lovely spring day.

chapter 3

Dom Broadley had watched from further along the nave as the girl left the abbey. He looked puzzled. Maybe he should have been a bit more sympathetic, he thought, when telling her about the mouse having eaten her cheese. But everything had happened so quickly that morning that he was still trying to get to grips with his own situation never mind having time to bother about a girl who walks into a tiny room and hundreds of black ravens fly out. Now that really had almost blown him away. He had thought his own situation was strange enough but that was something else. That beat the black dog appearing and whisking Dom back to the past any day. He was beginning to get used to that. But hundreds of black ravens? He shivered at the thought. And which century was he in this time? he wondered. What was he going to be involved in? Was the girl a part of it? He tried to place her clothes in history. Maybe the 16th Century? And certainly not high-status, as the archaeologists on the telly would say. A village girl, probably, and definitely not one of the fierce warriors of his last adventure back in time. Now that one had really been dangerous. Iona and Mull had definitely been the places to avoid if you fancied a quiet life back then. Was this girl from Iona or maybe the Ross of Mull? Bunessan? Lots of people lived there. But would that have been true in the girl's time? He knew he was about to find out for the black dog always came with a very definite agenda in mind and the girl's presence was not accidental, he was certain of that. He smiled to himself. Looked like this would be a piece of cake this time, much more peaceful and probably plain-sailing.

The girl was sitting on a small rocky outcrop by the shore. He walked over and sat down beside her. Dom Broadley did not believe in wasting time. Just get straight to the point, he thought. Set out your stall, that had always been his motto when he lived in Glasgow, and he saw no reason to change it now he was living for a time on Iona.
"Seems to me you're in a bit of bother. Need some help?" The girl eyed him keenly for a moment or two before making her decision. He felt like a kipper on a fishmonger's marble slab but he let her take her time. She was in big trouble and he felt sorry for her.
"Were you in the church?" she asked. He nodded.
"Yes."
"Did you hear what the monk said to me"? Dom liked her straight off for she, too, did not waste time.
"Yes, I did and I think you might just need some help and I seem to be the only person around who's not a monk and not tied to the abbey. The name's Dom.
"I'm Muirne. Thanks for the offer."

"So what's the plan?" he asked for he knew she would have thought of something already. She looked that kind of girl. Bossy - like himself.

"There is no plan. I think it's a quest. We travel and have to make sense of everything that will happen to us. Ask whoever we meet to tell us what the secret is."

"And get locked up for sounding really crazy," Dom added. Muirne laughed.

"Possibly. That's the problem, you see, we really only know very little. It will probably only unfold as we go along, - I hope," she added.

"And all has to be revealed before sunset," said Dom. Muirne sighed.

"I know, it sounds impossible but."

"But your mother is involved. I heard, so let's get a wiggle on. I take it we're heading for Mull."

"Yes. That boat's doing nothing." They looked at each other and smiled. Dom had the feeling they were going to get along really well. At last, a gentle type of mission this time.

"So it is. Lovely day for a sail."

Dom had never tried rowing a boat in his life. He had to force his legs to move nervously towards the small boat and wondered which end was the front.

"You actually have rowed before, haven't you?" asked Muirne, a horrible suspicion forming in her mind.

"Sure I have." How difficult could it be? "Right, you hop in and I'll push. Straight over to the other side, that do?" The surface of the blue waters of the Sound of Iona was barely disturbed by a gentle breeze. A piece of cake,

Tell me the Secret

thought Dom, his confidence returning. Muirne began dragging the light craft to the water's edge.

"I'll take one of the oars," she said. "The currents are very strong here and it's all affected by the state of the tide. If it's a spring tide today, there's no telling where we might end up."

"Rubbish! We'll skim across in no time. Jump in and we'll get cracking. Do you still have that bread and cheese?" They could always just break off the bit where the mouse had chewed. Dom was starving. Muirne nodded and climbed in.

"I was bringing it for my father. He's a stone-mason." Maybe it would be alright, she thought, casting a doubtful glance in Dom's direction. But he really did not look very comfortable near the boat. Still, she was used to sailing on Loch na Lathaich and she could take an oar, both even if necessary. Both would be better but it would hurt the boy's feelings and she did not want to do that. He did not have to help her. Dom's thoughts were somewhat different. He just hoped the girl could swim.

"We'll raise the sail," Muirne suggested. "There's a slight breeze coming from the west, so it will help push the boat along but not so strong as to let us lose control of it." Dom nodded and eyed the cloth-wrapped food parcel Muirne had placed on the wooden plank in front of the one they were both going to sit on.

"When we get there," he said, his voice sounding very loud in the near-total silence, "we can stop and have a bite to eat. It'll give us a chance to decide what to do next. The answers to your puzzle obviously don't lie here on Iona." Muirne agreed.

Tell me the Secret

"Tell me the secret. That's what the monk said I should ask."

"Ask who?" Muirne watched as Dom pushed the boat further into the water and then jumped in beside her. The boat dipped wildly as he did so and some of the bread landed in the water. Dom blushed and sat down carefully as the little boat finally settled on top of the glistening calm of the water. "Sorry about that," he said quietly and fumbled with the oar. "Maybe we'll get something to eat in your village later on," he suggested.

"There's still plenty for us in my bag," said Muirne glancing back at the island. She drew her breath in sharply. The landscape of Iona had changed. It was now unblemished by buildings of any description, no abbey, no nunnery and there would definitely be no village by the shores of Loch na Lathaich that she would recognise. No village would mean no people and no food. All would not yet exist for Muirne knew that she and Dom had walked through a time portal and back, maybe as much as a thousand years, into a world they knew nothing about. Still, maybe some people traded there by the loch and there were always berries a-plenty and fresh water to drink from Mull's countless tumbling fountains as they fell spectacularly from the high bens. They would survive - she hoped.

"Ask who?" Dom repeated.

"The monk didn't say." Dom's oar missed the water yet again. He hoped the girl had not noticed.

"Brilliant," said Dom, "he didn't 'do' conversation, did he?" After a few strokes, Dom finally got the hang of it and the boat moved quite steadily across the azure-blue water. The surface was calm and sparkling. Muirne's spirits lifted and despite the problems lying ahead of them, she felt convinced that with Dom's help, she would find out the secret that would bring her mother back home.

Muirne screamed! Dom dropped his oar into the water.

"Get it back! Hold on to the oar!" yelled Muirne as Dom hauled it back in.

"Hold on to anything!" he shouted back at her over the thundering storm that had come from out of nowhere. The rain lashed icy razors at them and the wind tossed the boat sky-high like a feather into the air. They hung there forever it seemed as the once-calm waters now boiled and bubbled far beneath them before the boat plunged uncontrollably into the raging torrent. They were soaked to the skin but by some miracle, the boat stayed upright after hitting the water at speed. The fall should have torn it apart but they had survived it. They hurtled along, driven recklessly by the wind and current. Muirne avoided looking at Dom's eyes and thought desperately of what to do to remain alive. Where had the roaring wind come from so suddenly? If it kept on blowing furiously, they would surely eventually capsize, maybe be driven into the cliffs on Mull's rocky shore or even something else that was almost too horrific to imagine, be swept south towards the fearsome Corryvreckan whirlpool. As long as they managed to keep the boat upright and to stay on board, they stood a slight chance of surviving. Dom was obviously no sailor so it would be up to Muirne to try to keep them alive. Yet again she wondered as they raced along where the wind had come from? And what was that screaming that was threatening to make her ears explode? A chilling folk-memory stole through her mind and she turned her gaze onto Dom to warn him to lower the sail as it was now billowing and being torn to shreds as the howling wind caught it and dragged the boat pitching recklessly along the boiling surface of the sea. But her words froze unspoken in her throat. Dom's face was petrified horror, his gaze fixed on something over her shoulder. That troubling memory finally burst into reality and she knew even before she turned to see what had virtually turned Dom to stone, what would be there. The Galkoni! She felt her energy drain away with the fear of it all. How many times had their hideous forms been spoken of round the village firesides, their evil deeds and merciless hounding of their victims recounted in hushed tones? But why us? Why Dom and me? She turned quickly before these thoughts had properly formed in her terrified mind. Horrible figures were whirling and diving around them, furiously trying to scratch them, tear at them, pull them out of the boat. Dom and Muirne scramble about to avoid their clutches in the pitching boat as the Golkani tried to wreck it and drown them in the boiling, foam-topped sea. Their eyes, quartered in different colours, spun constantly as their long green hair flew wildly in the gale. Their hands were longer than their short, stubby arms but ended in long tapering, spiky nails that had metal-tipped balls swinging lethally from them. They flashed past again and again as they attacked, the purple scales of their bodies darkening the air about them. Muirne pushed Dom down into the bottom of the boat and under the wooden seating for some protection. Perhaps then the demented creatures would fly away. No chance, though, she admitted to herself, but there was nothing else she could think of. At least if the boat capsized, they would not have themselves to blame. Dom now seemed transfixed, mesmerised by it all, unable to understand what was happening to him, unable to think. She knew he had no knowledge of creatures from the mists of time. His people had lost all folk memories so he had no idea how to combat such evil spirits. But Muirne had.

"Dom, your head, cover it! They'll go for your eyes!" Muirne knew that the only way to escape them was to dive underwater and hope to convince the Golkani that they had indeed drowned. She could not swim but she maybe Dom could. But he would be caught up in the strong current. There really was no way out, she admitted to herself, as she curled up in the bottom of the boat, the Golkani swooping and diving, screeching and screaming over the noise of the gale, desperately trying to claw at them, trying to force them to look into their kaleidoscopic eyes. But if they did that, Dom and Muirne would be lost forever. The little craft hurtled along and they expected it to flip over at any moment. They were drenched by the salt water, its taste a sickening gunge in their mouths. Their eyes were stinging as the bottom of the boat was constantly washed by sea water. But worst of all was the horrendous, shrill noise of the Golkani as they zipped through the turbulent air. It made their ears feel as if they were about to burst and seemed to freeze the blood in their veins. It never stopped. It just mingled with the raging storm as the boat dipped and rose in the frantic movements of the waves. The Golkani whirled and dipped, rose and plunged with them as they sensed their quarry might escape, getting more desperate as the moments passed. Dom made one desperate last bid to

Tell me the Secret

take down what was left of the sail as it was helping the fury of the wind drive them along. Muirne reached out to help him and then froze. Gorach! The Golkani leader! She knew a miracle was needed now. Dom looked helplessly at Muirne as Gorach's mighty form rose up from beneath the waters and towered before them. His long, green hair streamed out behind him as he hung in the air, his long, flowing robe of reddish brown clasped tightly at his waist with a jewelled belt of thick silver mesh. His eyes flickered like tongues of fire and his small, mean mouth showed teeth of sparkling rubies when he smiled at his victims. In his left hand, he carried a dirk of polished silver, a dirk whose tip held the white heat of a thousand fires within it. Gorach whirled the dirk around his head three times before finally launching it at the boat which would instantly dissolve in flames at its touch. They were doomed. It flew towards them at an incredible speed.

"Got it!" Dom screamed the news to Muirne above the high-pitched clamouring. He had managed to grab it by its jewelled handle as it flew past.

"Keep it! Don't throw it into the waves! Keep it!" shouted Muirne.

"I don't think I can hold it! It's trying to get free!" Dom shouted but his words were carried away and the breath knocked out of him by a monster wave. Gorach had lost his magical dirk and bellowed his threat of revenge before plunging once more beneath the boiling waves. Dom felt himself almost pitched into the water as Muirne grabbed for the dirk. She thrust it into her father's pitcher of ale and slammed in the stopper. Dom struggled in the bottom of the boat for breath and watched as Muirne struggled to open the pitcher once more.

"Camomile and lavender," she cried as she thrust the herbs inside the pitcher alongside the dirk. She jammed the stopper on again as tightly as possible. "The mixture will make it sleepy. It won't trouble us as long as it's sleepy." Dom nodded and wondered if it really mattered any more for the little craft was now being battered relentlessly by the Golkani and the storm. Both Muirne and Dom knew that they were destined to be battered on the rocks. Dom tried not to look at Muirne. There was now nothing they could do but wait as the waves and spray lashed over them. The sail was trashed, the oars lost. The boat was at the mercy of the elements. A smothering darkness fell over everything but the Golkani continued to try to claw them out of their tiny craft. Suddenly the boat seemed to slither to a halt.

"We're on the rocks," screamed Dom above the racket about them and then he heard it. The sound was so quiet he should not have been able to hear it. Muirne was laughing softly.

"No we're not," she said scornfully, "we've beached on the sands at Ardalanish. We've been driven past the cliffs. But quick. Get out before another wave draws us back again and keep low so that we're not spotted by the Golkani. Now run for it. Get in among the old bracken." Dom jumped out after Muirne and waded ashore as fast as he could. Suddenly the storm abated and all was silent and still.

chapter 4

Muirne lay exhausted among the bracken. The sun was beating down strongly and she felt it drying her clothes. There was no time, though, to rest. A dense, black cloud was gathering on the horizon. Dom stood looking at the empty beach.

"Our boat's a goner, Muirne. I think we're in for another storm." Muirne jumped up quickly, grabbing her hemp bag and leather pitcher as she did so.

"Those aren't rain clouds, Dom. That's the Golkani. They're massing to search for us. Move! Over there! Under the cliff! There are small caves there. We'll wait in one until it's safe to move on. Grab a few strong bits of driftwood as you go," she shouted as she raced along. "We'll need them if the Golkani spot us. Gorach will never stop trying to get his dirk back. It's also his wand of office. It lets everyone know he's the leader, the chief."

"Let's all the Golkani know who's boss, does it?" Dom was running along behind her as fast as he could. They both ran like the wind for cover and Muirne hoped the Golkani had not yet sent out lone scouts ahead of the main party. But the sky was clear overhead, a deep blue now and the air was fresh and calm. All was still on the land and she realised that the terrible storm had only taken place around them. It had been conjured up by Gorach and his Golkani

Tell me the Secret

to drown them. It was the sort of thing he did for fun. But now they had the dirk, he would not leave them alone. Muirne knew they would need all the help they could get if they were to seek out the answer to the question 'Tell me the secret' and bring her mother home again. The dirk had fantastic properties and there was no way she was going to give it up until her mother was safely home again. The first thing she must do was to gather a good supply of any kind of herb that would keep the dirk quiet until she needed it.

The cool, almost chilly air of the cave seemed to hit them full blast as they threw themselves into its dark safety.
"How long do you think they'll search hereabouts?" asked Dom edging closer to the mouth of the cave.
"Till they're satisfied we've not escaped. But don't raise your hopes," said Muirne. Dom watched as the horizon seemed to rise up and approach at an incredible speed, a terrible sound beginning to hum in his ears.
"They'll go away if they think we've drowned?" Dom suggested hopefully. Muirne shook her head.
"They'll go but they'll be back at some point. Of the Golkani, only Gorach can enter the water and live for he's really of another race. They always choose their leader from a race who are equally at home on land and sea. He will be scouring the sea bed right now for signs of us and he won't be satisfied with bits of a wrecked boat. To make it worse, we have Anluann."
"Who?"
"Anluann, the dirk. That's it's name. Don't say it aloud for he'll wake up and try to get out. We just might need his services. We'll free him when we've learned the secret. He'll be quite happy to sleep for a few hours. It won't do

him any harm. But once Gorach realises we've escaped, his anger will be truly terrible. Giving Anluann back now won't make any difference." Muirne tried hard to keep her voice steady, tried not to show how frightened she really was. "Can you see anything, Dom? Are they coming?" she asked quietly. He nodded, his voice a little unsteady when he spoke.

"Best we stay right back, behind those large boulders. The blackness back there should help. Is Anluann sound asleep?" They would need complete silence so that the Golkani would think the cave deserted if they discovered it. The huge granite boulders would look like the back wall of the cave in the complete blackness inside.

"I've put in more than enough herbs to keep him fast asleep for quite a while. If he were awake, he'd recognise their screeches and try to get back to them."

"Hope he doesn't snore," said Dom looking steadily at the small flask- like pouch. "Right, Muirne, here they come. Get right down flat in the hollow beneath that one and I'll do the same here."

"Dom, no matter what you hear, don't move," Muirne warned him. "They'll try every trick they know to lure us out. Stay completely still and silent and that way we'll be safe. They'll move on when they're satisfied the cave is empty."

They could hear the air outside begin to shake with the ominous sound of crazy, frantic screaming and wailing until it seemed to fill every inch of space in the cave. Dom could not see Muirne it was so dark inside. His stomach threatened to rumble. He swallowed hard to stop it and hoped to forget how hungry he was. Maybe they would not

Tell me the Secret

spot the cave opening, maybe they would fly right by. That hope died immediately. The Golkani were upon them! He could see their ghastly forms in his mind's eye, see their purple, scaly skin, their multi-coloured revolving eyes. He shut his own eyes as tightly as he could. He heard their screams of frustration as they raced wildly around the cave in their desperate search, their orange cloaks slicing the air about him. Suddenly, all was silent. But Dom remembered Muirne's warning and stayed exactly where he was. She would know when it was safe. She knew these creatures from a bygone age. How she had that knowledge he neither understood nor cared. Her understanding of them and their ways was their only hope of staying alive. He hoped with all his heart that she was still nearby, that they had not discovered her and carried her off. He waited, all thoughts of hunger completely forgotten. If they had her, how would she ever discover the secret and free her mother? Would Dom have to do it for her? Panic started to fill the space in Dom's stomach.

"Dom?" The soft sound was scarcely more than a whisper but it made Dom smile with relief.

"Ready to move on, Muirne?" he said brightly as if he had known all along that she was safe. "We really need to eat." His stomach really did rumble this time.

"You're right, of course, but we must remember the quest must be completed before sunset this evening. There are lots of berries we can collect as we go along but first we must find somewhere we can't be harmed by the Golkani."

"Berries! I was thinking about some crisps," said Dom.

"Crisps?"

Tell me the Secret

"Little slices of potato that. Never mind. I'll explain later. Do you know somewhere the Golkani won't see us while we try to find out more about the secret? They are definitely getting in the way," Dom complained.

"They will always find us," sighed Muirne, " because we must go out into the open at some point. But they've moved on further south and the one place we'll be truly safe from them is straight inland from here - only a journey of about a few miles. At the standing stones. They've been here since time began, I think, and they're sacred to humans and creatures alike." Dom had heard all about standing stones at school. Hadn't they something to do with the moon? Or was it the sun? He could not remember.

"Are they magic?" he asked, his curiosity well and truly roused.

"Perhaps. Nobody knows but the Golkani always steer clear of them, I'm sure of that. There is a sacred circle round the stones that they won't enter. It will give us time to eat and work out what to do next in safety. Until we have to move again," Muirne added, "for we'll be out in the open."

"In the forest would be safer," Dom suggested, "for I'm right in thinking they can't fly in dense woodland. Yes?" Muirne nodded in agreement.

"Absolutely correct," she said. But the bare, grassy land about them was covered in scrub and only a few sparse oaks were growing here and there. "There are lots of patches of forest but not right here and we don't know the best direction to take to find out the secret. We must think this out."

"So the standing stones it is. You're certain the Golkani won't approach us?"

"Yes. But we must get there first. We must eat when we can, Dom, for we've no idea where this quest will lead us."

"I've got this we could share," said Dom pulling a mouldy-looking breakfast bar from his pocket.

"What's that?" asked Muirne, a look approaching horror on her small elfin-shaped face.

"You're supposed to eat it. It's food. I know it's rather crushed, a bit soggy and covered in fluff where the wrapper has come away but, like it says on the wrapper, it's very nutritious. See, blueberries, raspberries, oats - just like porridge - hardly any salt. Actually it tastes vile but, as it says on the label, it's good for you and helps the poor because the maker give some money to them. Keeps most of it himself, I can't deny that. Want some?" He gently teased a bit of fluff off it and offered it to Muirne.

"I'll stick to fresh berries but thanks all the same. There are plenty of them just outside. Wait here." She edged closer to the mouth of the cave, Dom following silently behind. With every movement, they expected to hear the thundering, awful tones of Gorach. Muirne stopped and suddenly a cold chill swept over both of them. A shadow fell across the mouth of the cave. Dom pulled Muirne back, his heart pounding, his mouth completely dry. The sun behind the tall, slender figure meant Muirne and Dom could not see the woman's face. She turned slightly and sunlight flooded over her. Dom's heart rate slowed to normal immediately for the young woman's smile was gentle and friendly. Her voice was sweet and soft when she spoke.

Tell me the Secret

"I am Mariota, a daughter of Fionn mac Cumhaill." Fionn mac Cumhaill, the legendary Celtic hero. Even Dom had heard of him. This lady was a kind of princess. Wow! Muirne was entranced by her long, pale hair that seemed to fall as if a silver waterfall down her back. The long, green tunic over a deep blue dress seemed to shimmer in the morning light as the gold threads running through it caught the sun's rays. You will need both of these." The long, gold-edged sleeves glittered as she reached out to Muirne. In her hands she held two small, pale brown pouches. "Take this one, Muirne."

"Thank you. What's in them?" asked Muirne quietly as she took them.

"All the berries and seeds you will need for you have very little time left to discover the secret and no time to go gathering these. It must be discovered before sunset or all is lost for you and me. This will save you precious time. No more need now to search for food. Take this one," she said to Dom. "These are herbs needed for keeping Gorach's dirk, Anluann, quiet." Dom had had enough of that dirk.

"Why don't we just throw it away. I know Muirne thinks." He stopped speaking as Mariota put up her hand to silence him.

"Listen to Muirne, Dom, and be guided by her instincts." She placed the cord attached to the leather pouch round his neck. "Muirne is right. Anluann will always find its way back to Gorach and he only uses its powers to destroy. Muirne will use them for good not evil." Mariota! At the back of his mind, somewhere, Dom was sure he had heard that name before. Muirne had frowned a little, too, when she had heard it, he was almost sure of that.

Tell me the Secret

"So Gorach would use the dirk to destroy Muirne and me," said Dom. Mariota nodded.

"You have seen him try that already. That is his intention. He will find you eventually and you will need all the help you can get. There are ways of using Anluann against him but I cannot tell you what they are for it will make them useless. You have to discover them for yourselves. Just keep it with you until you have no more need of it." Dom put his arm through the leather tie and thought it would be more secure slung across his body. Mariota nodded in approval.

"Do you know the secret, Mariota? Can't you tell us?" pleaded Muirne. Mariota! That was the name carved on the stone by her father just a few weeks ago. Odd, thought Muirne, but obviously just a coincidence. That was a thousand years into the future.

"Muirne, only you can make the final connection that will reveal the secret. I can only help by telling you that there will be four answers and only when they rest together as one will the spell be broken."

"What spell?" asked Dom.

"The one that holds Muirne's mother apart from her family."

"And we only have till sunset?" said Dom.

"Yes. Now make ready to leave," said Mariota.

"Will we see you again?" asked Muirne hopefully.

"Yes and very soon for we have no time now to speak. But I can't solve the puzzles you will meet on your quest. It has to be you, Muirne. Take care, both of you." Muirne glanced at Dom and when she looked back, Mariota had vanished.

"She sounded very wise," said Dom wishing the woman had stayed to help.

"She is. She's a drui-ban - a wise woman. She understands both worlds."

"Both?" asked Dom puzzled.

"This one and the world of nature, spirits, gods and heroes unseen by the rest of us."

"A witch?"

"Are you listening, Dom? I said a wise woman, a keeper of the ancient knowledge and ways. Now, if Mariota, daughter of the great Fionn mac Cumhaill, says we're to move, then that's what we're going to do."

"Where to?"

"One of the most sacred places on the island, the two ancient standing stones not far from here. I've already explained all this. You're too busy thinking of your stomach to listen. Now move. You can eat that ghastly thing while we go."

"But what makes them so sacred?" asked Dom ignoring the last insult.

"They contain vast amounts of knowledge. Something to do with their position. But the main quality they have that's important to us is that they scare the living daylights out of Gorach and his fiendish friends."

"Is there really something that vile Gorach fears?" asked Dom cautiously approaching the mouth of the cave.

"Gorach will definitely be afraid since he no longer has his precious dirk. We must make sure we keep it with us always," said Muirne firmly.

"So it's four answers that we're after - four mini-quests," Dom suggested.

Tell me the Secret

"Unless this is already part of the first."

"And how will we know, Muirne?"

"We'll know if we get the answer to our question. 'Tell me the secret.' Sounds simple enough but what we don't know is if the answer will come from friend or foe."

"As I see it, Muirne, we're a bit short of friends right now so any answers we might get could quite easily come from Gorach's mates and that will definitely lead us to our own destruction." Muirne shook her head decisively.

"We have to use our own judgment in this. I have every faith in mine." Dom noticed Muirne made no mention of his. "Now, let's move out of this cave. We've no time to lose."

"Lead the way, Muirne. Don't worry. I'm sure between us we'll get it solved. We're a team."

"Yes, Dom, we're in this together and I really do thank you for coming on this quest with me."

"So what are we hanging about here for? Time to get your mum and dad back where they belong."

chapter 5

They ran swiftly and silently from the cave and Dom expected Gorach's terrifying voice to split the air at any moment. But nothing happened. He heard only the gentle breaking of the waves on the Ardalanish sands. Relief surged through him. Muirne raced ahead of him as they climbed up the slopes bordering the sea and onto the flatter land above.

"Do you think they're still searching for us, Muirne?" he called as she stopped several metres ahead of him.

"They probably think we've been swept south towards the whirlpool."

"They might think we've drowned in it then? Even Gorach won't dive into that?" Dom suggested hopefully.

"I think so but we can't be sure. We'll make for the standing stones, the bigger of the two, and that will give us time to think out some kind of plan for they'll never dare to come too close."

"Too scared," Dom suggested.

"Yes. They'll have one last look into all the caves around here, examine every last spot in them, and they're bound to have a look at the stones too." They both looked round at the surrounding landscape and knew that there was very little cover nearby. The Golkani would be upon them before they would ever be able to reach the forest they could see in the distance. Muirne's spirits plummeted. She recognised almost nothing. There were no familiar farm buildings, no cottages and no sign at all of St Ernan's where she had last seen her father. All of it had gone and the land was as it had probably looked more than a thousand years before. She knew then that if there was a small settlement where Bunessan had been, it would probably be no more than a few cottages, completely unrecognisable to her. She would know nobody. How could they expect help from complete strangers if they needed it?

"There they are!" shouted Dom although by now he was right beside her.

"I see them," she said. In the distance, Muirne could make out the dark outline of the two standing stones clearly etched against the deep blue sky. Only a few miles of lush grass and easy terrain lay between Dom, Muirne and the ancient, mysterious stones. Dom shuddered and wondered who had placed them there. Were they watching them at that very moment? "Now move, Dom." Muirne hurried on as she spoke and crossed the ground swiftly and silently, her feet in their soft leather shoes hardly seeming to touch the ground beneath them. Dom's trainers crunched solidly as he tried to keep up with her, every step he took seeming to echo so loudly he was sure the Golkani would swoop down on them shrieking and clawing before they reached the safety of the stones.

"Look!" Muirne stopped once more, her gaze fixed on something a short distance in front of them.

"What's up?" Dom peered into the bright sunshine and could just make out an object, bright and sparkling on the calm blue waters of a small river. "What is it?"

"A boat." Dom looked at her. He knew he had excellent eyesight but somehow Muirne seemed to see things long before he did.

"That? But it's odd, really weird if it is," he said. "Okay, the shape sort of resembles one but only just. Doesn't look like any boat I've ever seen before." Muirne nodded.

"That's just because it's not made of any material people usually use. It's made of glass, crystal, in fact."

"That's impossible. Nobody could make a glass boat that big. It's twice the size of the one we lost. And why would they have such an exotic craft just to sail it up and down a river that size? Wooden ones are a lot easier and cheaper. I don't know much about boats but it can't be easy to control, slithering about all over the place. It's probably just a wooden one that's had a few coats of sparkly paint." Muirne laughed.

"You just don't understand, Dom, do you?"

"Understand what?" he asked.

"What's just happened to us. You're talking as if we were not in Tir Tairngiri."

"Where?" Muirne sighed before replying.

"Tir Tairngiri. The Land of Promise. In these other worlds, anything is possible. We are completely defenceless here. Haven't you realised that yet? People can turn themselves into different creatures or even trees and streams or."

"Boats," suggested Dom sarcastically.

"Maybe. I don't know." Muirne shrugged and looked again at the boat.

"Maybe that crystal boat is really somebody's granny." Muirne refused to smile. Dom shook his head and wondered why she believed in all of this. He had conveniently forgot about Mariota and Gorach and the Golkani. But Muirne had not.

"Think back," she said, "think Golkani. They aren't just something you imagined, are they? Something you saw in a nightmare? Dom, they are real for Tir Tairngiri is the world they inhabit. Gorach rose up out of the sea - a creature who took the form of a man. He then dissolved before our eyes. They are real, Dom, very real and their main aim right now is to destroy us. When they've done that, they'll move onto some other creatures and do the same all over again just for more fun. In this land, Dom, believe nothing you see and nothing that you are told. Suspect everything. Be aware that here humans have no friends, just enemies. One slip and we could be destined to roam the earth forever, seeing our friends and families but not able to touch them or speak to them."

"I'll be careful, Muirne, I promise you that. I'll do nothing careless that will harm us." Dom felt frightened at the very thought of never being part of his family again. "I'm sure we'll be alright," he added for he certainly hoped so. But time was running out. The sun had already passed the midday height. "What next?" he asked.

"To get to the standing stones, we must cross the river. It's not wide as you can see but it's deep. It is shallower farther up but we could lose precious minutes going that way. This is the most direct route."

"Then we'll have to cross in that boat for I don't see a bridge."

"It looks like it's just been abandoned. I can't see anybody nearby. The land around is all open," said Muirne, her keen eyes carefully examining every little hillock.

Tell me the Secret

"Safe then?" asked Dom.

"Completely," said Muirne. If Muirne was satisfied then so was Dom. They checked on the dirk before moving off. "I'll have to crush some more lavender when we stop. It's more effective that putting the seeds in whole. I think Anluann is beginning to wake up."

"I'll take him and check up on it properly when we stop. You've got enough to carry, Muirne. I promise I'll be very careful. We want to use it, not to be destroyed by it," said Dom.

"It'll all be over by sunset - one way or the other," added Muirne ominously. "So let's hurry on down to the river. If we only knew exactly how to find the answers to that question. We're sort of working in the dark here. There's nobody that I can see about here so how can we possible ask someone who doesn't exist?" said Muirne. Dom hurried on beside her and they ran quickly down to the river's edge.

"Why on earth would anyone want to own a crystal boat?" he wondered aloud. "And how can we possible row it? There are no oars in it and nothing we can use lying about. No poles we could even use to push it across using the river bed. I wish we'd brought the driftwood we picked up on the beach to defend ourselves against the Golkani." For once, Muirne seemed baffled.

"But how did it get here?" she wondered softly.

"How did what get here?" croaked a voice behind them. Dom and Muirne both turned sharply. An old woman sat by the stream looking forlorn, a pile of washing in a large, wooden tub beside her. They looked at each other and Dom felt a cold tingle run down this spine. The sooner they reached the safety of the standing stones, the better. Muirne seemed to be thinking the same thing and they both began to turn towards the boat. It had vanished! Dom looked at Muirne but she had already moved away and had sat down beside the old woman as if nothing strange had happened. The old woman eyed her slyly. Muirne just smiled sweetly.

"We have some fresh berries. Would you like some?" she asked the old woman. The woman shook her head and pulled a face.

"I'd rather have some help wringing these blankets," she said, "for I'm not as young as I used to be and my hands won't wring the water from them as they used to. I don't know how I'll manage." Dom stepped in.

"I'll do it for you," he offered, "you just have something to eat."

"Leave it, Dom," said Muirne sharply. But Dom had already begun to twist the cloth with his hands.

"Dear," said the old woman turning to Muirne, "I'd like some blaeberries. There are some bushes up on the hill. They're always first to ripen. It's been a long time since I tasted blaeberries because my old legs can't climb like they used to. Would you be a kind girl?" She smiled a toothless grin that sent shivers down that same spine. Muirne smiled kindly.

"Of course I'll fetch you some. I'll do it right away. Dom, you come too," urged Muirne as she ran lightly up the bank.

"Doesn't need the two of us," he shouted after her. He was going nowhere. That boat had to be somewhere and he was determined to track it down. Had it drifted out of sight behind the bushes at the bend in the river? he wondered, still wringing the water from the cloth. And there was also that question they had to ask. Since the old woman seemed to be the only person around, maybe she was the one with the answer, he thought. He would stay there while Muirne collected the berries and winkle it out of the old woman.

"Dom, come on!" shouted Muirne yet again. What was her problem? he wondered beginning to get a bit irritated. There was no way he was leaving now that he had made his plans.

"I'll wait here and help with the sheets," he called to Muirne. "Be quick! When you reach the top of the hill," he shouted, "see if you can spot the crystal boat."

"Dom, get up here!" Dom was becoming exasperated with Muirne. He ignored her this time and smiled at the old woman. He was sure she must have seen what had happened to the boat and he was determined to stay there until he found out. The boat was their best hope.

chapter 6

"Is your friend afraid to be on her own? Has something frightened her?" asked the old woman.

"Our boat was wrecked and I suppose she's still a bit shaken. We almost drowned," explained Dom.

"She reminds me of my grand-daughter. She usually helps me but she's gone down to the shore with her friends. I just need another pair of hands for a little while, that's all."

"Did you see where that boat went?" asked Dom, wringing out all the water from a large sheet as best he could.

"What boat?"

"The one that was here when my friend and I came along."

The old woman nodded.

"Oh, that one. That's a tidal river there, you know. If the undercurrent catches anything. Well, you know how strong the pull is," said the old woman shaking her head at past memories. Dom nodded. He certainly knew all about the currents hereabouts. A sudden thought struck him.

"Do you think it's maybe just round the bend in the river? Maybe resting against the bank?" he suggested hopefully.

"You're probably right. It will have been snagged on that rotten tree trunk that drifted down from up river last winter. Only fish can come and go in these waters without a bit of help. When you've finished wringing that out, dear, perhaps you could help me lay it out on the bushes to dry. Want some bread? Freshly made by me this morning.

Crusty. Just the way the family like it." Dom smiled at the very thought of something to eat at last. He took the chunk offered and sat down, his back against a black, rocky outcrop. The sun was now beating down and he was glad of the cooling water the old woman had poured into a tiny wooden beaker for him from her leather flask. He looked back up the hill but Muirne was nowhere to be seen.

"That would have been too much for you to do by yourself," he said sleepily.

"I'll have a few choice words to say to that grand-daughter of mine when she turns up wanting her supper, I can tell you. Now, just this sheet over the bushes and that's me done for the day. It'll dry in no time and it can be collected this evening." The old woman eased herself up onto her feet, groaning a little as she did so. Dom squinted at her through the bright, slanting rays of the sun. He felt tired and very sleepy. Maybe he could persuade Muirne to stay here for a while when she returned. He sat up suddenly but fell back onto his elbows. That was ridiculous. They had no time to lose. But he felt so very tired and his legs felt like lead. The ground seemed to be moving beneath him. Had he actually been asleep? He had not felt the least bit tired before he helped the old woman. In the distance, he could see Muirne racing towards him, could see himself seeming to float along on the top of the water but felt dry as a bone.

"Get out! Get out, Dom!" Muirne's shouts were coming at him through the gentle movement of the water, through a haze of sun and sky and a hard, ice-cold surface that glistened beneath him. Not water, not the river. But the boat, the beautiful, crystal craft he lay in as it took him to -

Tell me the Secret

where? To another world? Dom shook his head violently and tried desperately to throw off this awful tiredness and the leaden feeling in his legs. He knew then that the boat had never vanished. It was another manifestation of the old woman and she was taking him where he would be lost forever, for all eternity.

"Muirne," he muttered feebly, "help me."

"Dom, get out!" Muirne was much closer now but he was trapped - just like Anluann. The sleeping draught must have been in that drink the old woman had given him. He could hear Muirne's voice very clearly and turned his head towards the sound, but try as he might, he could barely get his elbows to support him as he tried to sit up in the bottom of the boat. Was it moving faster now, he wondered, and the seeds of panic began to grow in his mind. He had to do as Muirne had said. Somehow he had to get out. But he would drown if he toppled the boat for his limbs refused to obey his brain. He would not be able to swim. He heard a cackling, triumphant sound and he was sure the old woman was in that boat with him although he could not see her. He knew then that she was once more part of the crystal structure. She would never let him go.

"Muirne, I can't!" His voice sounded shrill and panicky on the hot, still air. "I can't," he cried once more. She was still racing alongside, trying to keep up although her legs were being deeply scratched by the gorse.

"You know what you have to do. The old woman is Deoca. She is evil. The crystal is part of her. Hurry before it's too late," Muirne was shouting, " for she lures people to her world and they can never return." Now Muirne was ahead of them for she knew the boat would slow down as it took

Tell me the Secret

the bend. She hoped it might be pushed over by the current nearer the bank. Perhaps she could then reach out and grab it until Dom could pitch himself into the water. She would then be able to haul him over to the safety of the bank. Dom knew then that there was nothing that could stop the boat sailing on for all eternity once they had rounded the bend in the river. Muirne was right. He knew exactly what he had to do. Anluann was in its waterproof pouch now inside the pocket of his joggies for safety. Dom's strength was gradually returning in his hands and feet. No time to wait. Dom felt for the dirk, hiding his movements as best he could. He guessed the old crone was now disguised as the rudder for it was guiding the boat to the open sea. He could see its movements as they avoided small rocks and floating debris. Slowly, agonisingly slowly, he edged his fingers till he finally felt the cold metal. Suddenly the rudder stopped moving. Dom hurled Anluann towards it but it was deflected from its target as an arm shot up before him. Dom tried to grab the crone's tunic but only a button came away as she shook herself free of him. The old woman screamed a sound of fury that chilled Dom's very blood as the dirk woke up on impact with the arm. It hurled itself at what remained of the now vanishing crystal craft and flew in an uncontrollable rage at the old woman. She had emerged fully as her old self but now vanished. Anluann fizzled, puzzled, into the water as Dom floundered helplessly alongside it. He tried to swim but his legs still were not strong enough and he sank heavily into the soft bed of the fast-flowing current as the water closed over him. The cold water seemed to fill his mouth, ears, nose and even his very eyes as he lay there helplessly. Suddenly he was

Tell me the Secret

catapulted into the air and dragged along the river before being hauled onto the clawing muck of the river bank.

"You might at least try to help. I can't do everything around here, you know. Drink this. Make it quick for we've lost a lot of time thanks to you and your need to be seen as everybody's friend." Dom's head was roughly jerked back by his hair and Muirne poured a brew down his throat. "Aagh!" she screamed, "what's that in your hair? Slime? How revolting," she said her eyes narrowing in disgust. "Wash it out." She looked at her hands and quickly took her own advice. Dom blushed faintly.

"It's only hair gel," he protested as the brew worked and his strength began to return.

"What? You actually put that on your hair?" Dom felt ever so slightly embarrassed.

"Never mind that! I'm suffering here, you know," he complained. "A bit of sympathy wouldn't go amiss. I only got myself involved in all of this as a favour to you and all I get is abuse. I've half a mind to chuck the whole business and go home. At least I'll get something decent to eat there. Crisps or something," he added although he didn't really like crisps. He was not much of a savouries kind of guy. A nice cupcake would do the trick and maybe a sausage roll.

"What? Well, whatever it is, you can forget it. Your only way back is through me. We're in this together whether we like it or not and from now on, I'll keep Anluann." Dom watched as she carefully checked that the dirk was once more drowsy and happy. How on earth had she got hold of it? Dom wondered. He thought he had lost it forever in the river but he was determined not to admit it.

"Where's the old woman?" asked Dom looking about him. The river flowed by peacefully as if nothing at all had happened. "She tried to kidnap me. Had me down as her slave for life probably."

"Her name's Deoca. I recognised her straight off. Four fingers on one hand, three on the other. Didn't you notice?" asked Muirne. "Alright, I'll admit it. I couldn't place her at first but it seemed to ring a bell somewhere at the back of my mind. By the way, life in her world means forever and a day and she doesn't go in for slaves. She would have married you off to one of her relatives. Must be a bit of a shortage in Tir nam Ban - Land of Women," she explained. Muirne tried hard not to laugh as she teased Dom. Dom ignored that remark.

"What really happened anyway? What was that all about?" he asked as the feeling in his body began to return.

"The old tales tell of a crone who lurks by rivers and lures travellers into her clutches before taking them to her world. She can change shape at will but always into something to do with water. A seal, a kelpie or."

"A crystal boat."

"Exactly. Something she thinks the traveller might be particularly interested in," Muirne explained. "As soon as she appeared and the boat seemed to have vanished, I had a very bad feeling about it."

"And that was the reason you didn't want me to help her?" Muirne nodded.

"But did you listen to me, Dom? Did you forget what Mariota said about trusting my instincts?" Muirne looked up at the sun. "We'd best get moving."

Tell me the Secret

"Muirne, I just thought you were anxious to reach the standing stones. I didn't think she was maybe some mythical creature."

"Obviously. Well, it doesn't matter now. The boat has sailed away. Deoca will have to do a bit of first-aid where Anlunna scorched through her dozens of layers of clothing when she gets home and becomes herself once more. I think we've seen the last of her."

"She gave me some delicious home-made bread," said Dom still aware of his rumbling stomach.

"And a lovely cool drink, I expect," Muirne suggested. Dom nodded.

"It was drugged, wasn't it," he said as the truth suddenly dawned on him.

"Yes."

"It made me feel so tired, Muirne. I could hear you calling but I was just too tired to do what you were telling me to do."

"Oh, don't bother about that. It all went really well. I'm very happy about it," she said smiling at Dom.

"Happy that I nearly drowned, was nearly kidnapped."

"Yes, for it gave me the chance to sort out Deoca while you were enjoying yourself drifting along on the current. Anluann was thrashing about in a terrible temper so I just picked him up and threatened Deoca with him as she tried to cool her arm down in the water. Did you realise you'd lost him and his little water-bed? No?"

"You did what?"

"I asked her to tell me the secret or I'd let Anluann loose. So she told me." Muirne sighed. "Makes no sense, though.

Tell me the Secret

All she said was, 'I begin at the end.' Still, maybe once we put it altogether it will become clear."

"She just said 'I begin at the end.'?"

"Just that. Now, come on. We've over half a mile to go and time is quickly vanishing." They climbed the bank onto the higher ground. They would have to go the longer way now that they had no boat. Muirne's eyes glanced seaward and Dom set off fast without looking. He knew what she must have seen from the changed expression on her face. Gorach and the Golkani were massing again on the horizon. He knew that from the fear in Muirne's eyes. Dom hoped they would make it to the safety of the sacred circle but what then? There was so much to do, so many secrets still to discover and they could achieve nothing if they were penned into that small space until sunset. Right then they stood to lose their freedom forever. But Muirne would think of something, wouldn't she? He raced after her over the uneven grassy mounds, tripping and stumbling in his haste, Muirne flying along with the slight breeze spilling out her red-gold hair behind her.

"Dom!" she called back to him, "whatever happens to me, just keep on running. Mariota will help you if you are alone. Don't stop for anything. You have to get there, you have to reach the standing stones." Dom could not reply for he felt his lungs were bursting with the effort of trying to keep up with her. He staggered crazily as his leg was ripped by a sharp rock, quickly regained his balance and kept on going as fast as he could. He could hear the screeching and screaming of the Golkani, hear Gorach's war cry fast approaching but kept his panic in check and his eyes on Muirne's back. Suddenly Muirne fell to the ground and

Dom stumbled over her and into something very hard. The standing stone! They had made it. But would they ever be able to leave?

chapter 7

The Golkani swooped and tore at the ground centimetres from Muirne and Dom then soared off and settled some twenty metres away on a grassy outcrop. Dom lay panting, his back as close to the taller of the two stones as he could get without touching the sacred object. That it was definitely sacred he had gathered from the way Muirne looked at it in wonder. Gorach stood among his followers, magnificent, imposing and threatening. His gaze never wavered for a second from the lovely, slender figure of the tall, graceful woman who stood with her left hand resting lightly on the top of the taller stone. Mariota had come and Gorach was treating her with the greatest caution. Her long, flaxen hair now fell like a sparkling, shimmering fountain down her back to her waist. The green velvet of her tunic with its golden cord around it looked like a magical forest with a narrow path winding through it. She smiled sweetly, her eyes half-closed but with a veiled threat in them as she looked at Gorach. He finally dropped his gaze among the quiet cursing and mutterings of the spiteful Golkani fluttering around him. The young woman laughed softly and looked down at Muirne and Dom.

"Ignore them," she said in her quiet voice. "They will stay where they are while you are within the circle around the sacred stones. The stones will always protect the good and punish the evil among us. The Golkani are vicious and Gorach is headstrong, but also cunning and dangerous." Mariota remained standing and almost seemed to be a part of the stone pillar itself.

"Who put these stones here?" Dom blurted out without thinking.

"People like you and Muirne but they were much closer to the rhythm of the land, the seas and the heavens with all their stars and the sun and the moon." Mariota's own long dress beneath the green tunic was of a deep, blue hue and spoke of moonlight when matched with her flaxen hair. Murine sat on the grass looking almost transfixed by now being able to gaze upon a figure from the land and time of gods and heroes of the Celtic mist. Somehow, in the depths of her mind, she knew this was a day she had always known would come, a day in her life she would never know again, never speak of even once for no-one would believe her. Mariota had lived in a time almost forgotten and never really believed to have existed. But Muirne knew Mariota was real and would be alive until the end of time - somewhere. Now Mariota was smiling and the gold-threaded tassel of her belt swayed in the gentle breeze and brushed against Muirne's curly golden hair. Mariota's striking eyes, blue as the deepest night sky, now rested on Dom as she spoke once more. "Again I tell you to listen to Muirne for she has the gift." Both Muirne and Dom looked puzzled by this and Mariota laughed before she spoke again.

Tell me the Secret

"Just accept it, both of you. Use the gifts to solve the riddle," she added.

"Gorach won't try to attack us while you're here, Mariota, will he?" Dom wanted to know nothing of magical gifts whatever they were. Gorach was the real problem right then and he wanted a solution to that - and fast.

"Gorach's main destructive power lies in his command of Anluann. You are not safe from him while you still have it," Mariota said.

"Then we'll give it back to him." Dom always sought the simplest solution. Mariota sighed quietly.

"Of course you can do so if you wish. But if you do, you will lose all hope of rescuing your parents, Muirne. You will need its powers to take you safely to the end of your quest - to discover the secret. Besides, Gorach thinks you have insulted him, Dom. Even if he recovers Anluann, he will still seek revenge for being made to look foolish at being bettered in battle by a mere child."

"So it's a lose-lose situation," said Dom frowning. "Looks like we keep the dirk then. But Mariota, we know part of the secret already. We know one of the answers. That horrible old woman by the river told us, didn't she, Muirne?"

"That's right, she did, Mariota. It makes no sense to us, though," she said. "Please listen to what she said. 'I begin at the end.' That's all. Do you know what it means? Please tell us if you do," pleaded Muirne. Mariota shook her head as Muirne spoke and sent a shimmering wave of light flowing down her pale, silken hair.

"It's your quest, Muirne, no-one else's. Dom is allowed to help only because he knows nothing of the past."

Tell me the Secret

"But I don't either," protested Muirne. But Mariota seemed not to hear her. "The old woman's words. What do they mean? What are we supposed to do with her answer?"

"Keep it in your memory. It's just part of the answer. There's more to this secret, much more. This is a very complex riddle."

"Riddle?" echoed Dom.

"Yes and all four answers are needed before it is unlocked. And with the answers are four objects." Muirne and Dom looked at each other and Dom groaned. The whole thing was not complex, it was impossible. Dom had only just escaped with his life and that had only resulted in one tiny part of this riddle. It was just not going to happen. There was no way they could go on groping in the dark. Dom shook his head almost in defeat and plucked a long blade of grass as the silence around him lengthened. A sudden, dark murmuring grew and filled the air around them and he looked nervously towards where the Golkani had posted three scouts before the main body had retreated behind the knoll. Dom knew that Mariota and Muirne were watching him - Mariota interested in his reaction to the knowledge that real danger would face them again and again as they sought out the next three answers and objects. Was the button the first of these? Would he decided to go on? Muirne was waiting silently, knowing how much Dom had suffered at Deoca's hands and his determination not to repeat the experience. He looked over to where Mariota and Muirne waited. Mariota suddenly spoke again.

"Dom, you cannot give the dirk back and walk away. Gorach lost it in battle and must win it back the same way

Tell me the Secret

from the same opponent. That's you! There is really no way out of that."

"Three more answers?" asked Dom slowly looking first at Muirne and then at Mariota. "Where will we find them?" If he had to do battle with Gorach, he might as well make sure something good came out of the whole business. Muirne could be reunited with her parents. He could at least help her try to crack the code, so to speak.

"Dom, you don't have to do this," said Muirne, " really you don't. I can't even promise you anything to eat except berries."

"Love them," said Dom butting in quickly, " fantastic things, berries." All three of them burst out laughing. "We're a team, Muirne. I've always been a terrific team player." In Dom's heart of hearts he knew he was a very poor team player. Everybody said so. Too bossy. They said that as well. "So then, Mariota, where do Muirne and I start looking?" But Mariota slowly shook her head.

"That I can't tell you. Both of you already have all you need. It is all within your own power."

"But, Mariota," said Muirne, " you will be with us?" Mariota shook her head again.

"Nearby then," Dom suggested hopefully.

"Somewhere - perhaps. But I must go and you must hurry," she said.

"Will we feel you near, though, even if we don't actually see you," asked Muirne.

"Perhaps." Mariota's hand lightly brushed the sacred stone as she spoke. Dom looked once more towards the knoll and heard the sounds of movement behind it.

Tell me the Secret

"But we can't move from here. The Golkani are still over there. Help us, please," Dom pleaded. The air about them seemed to shimmer for a moment or two and then became still. Mariota was gone. Dom felt shattered.

"We have all that we need but that amounts to virtually nothing, Muirne. I have my torch, batteries dying fast. Actually, they're dead. Must have been knocked on during that struggle with Deoca," he said glumly.

"Here are the seeds, the herbs," said Muirne.

"And the words 'I begin at the end.' for what they're worth and a button. So what next, Muirne? Where to - always assuming there is a next place? Don't think that features in Gorach's plans for us. The minute we move away from the immediate vicinity of these stones, you and I, Muirne, are a pair of dead ducks." Muirne shook her head thoughtfully.

"I think it all has something to do with the Mariota stone back at St Ernan's. Listen, Dom, Mother was last seen sitting beside it and exactly one month later, Father vanishes while he's working on it. That must mean something."

"That's wonderful, Muirne. Just one little problem, though. The stone-slab isn't here for us to inspect, so if it contains any kind of secret, we'll never know before sunset. Even if we could get over to St Ernan's, we've gone right back through a time portal to an age long before your father worked on it. All his art will not have been chiselled onto it yet. A blank stone, nothing more." But Muirne was shaking her head as he spoke.

"Father didn't do the carving, only the writing, the inscription."

"Which said?" asked Dom

"'Here lies Mariota daughter of'. That's all so far. That's all I saw when I took his food to him this morning." Was it only this morning? Muirne wondered. "Nobody knows who did the designs or when." This time it was Dom who shook his head.

"Same problem It isn't here. We can't study them."

"Oh yes we can," said Muirne triumphantly. "We have one other thing here in my pouch. Father's plan of the stone and it includes the original Celtic designs. He'd left the parchment beside his tools. He had intended to incise a Celtic design round the edges when he'd finished the inscription and was going to trace the intertwining design on paper first to see how he could fit it all in. I thought it might blow away in the breeze and took it with me to Iona to give to him with his meal." Dom watched as Muirne spread the little roll of parchment out in the shadow of the tall, standing stone, his mind doing its best to blot out the increasing screeches of the hidden Golkani. Muirne and Dom both knew they could not remain there much longer for they needed strength from food and water if they were to have any chance of outwitting these vile creatures.

The Golkani had now moved back into sight. Gorach knew he could wait, knew time was on his side. The two children would have to risk everything soon and then they all knew they were doomed. As he sat on the greatest of the boulders that had seemingly been strewn about by giants of a past era, Gorach polished his shield till it dazzled onlookers in the rays of a sun that had already reached the top of its journey across the sky. He smiled to himself and watched with interest as a black mass seemed

to approach, slithering across the ground towards them. Rats. They always sensed when a feast was in the offing.
"Leave them alone," he ordered his restless Golkani sharply. "Let them finish off what we will begin."

Muirne looked closely at her father's drawings spread out before them and blinked back tears. The long, rectangle of granite bore the most beautiful swirling designs.
"There's father's stonemason's mark. The tiny raven. He always says he's descended from the Vikings. They always had that design on their ships. He hasn't cut it on the actual stone yet." Muirne's voice was thick with disappointment. "I was sure it would reveal something - be important though I can't now see how," she said beginning to roll the design up again very carefully. It was just a very small copy of the Mariota stone. It meant nothing to her. She did not even know who this other Mariota was. Nobody did yet. Perhaps it was a nun from Iona.
"Wait a minute, Muirne, don't be too hasty. Lay it out again. I've got a vague idea it all means something. If we just look at the basic three designs, the square and the two rectangles. You know something, I think this is a map. Hold it away from you a bit and let me see it. I'm right," Dom said excitedly, " that's exactly what it is. This is a map of some of the islands around here. I've seen it in the atlas in school."
"Atlas?" repeated Muirne puzzled.
"Drawings of places as if you were seeing them from above. As if you were a bird," he tried to explain. "But it's not the outside shape that's important, it's what is inside. Look, this square on it is Ulva with its woods and streams. Looks

Tell me the Secret

like a rose but it isn't and that raised blob in the middle must mean something very important. A place on the island maybe. Looks as if it's right in the very centre of the island. We'll study the others later and work out which ones they are. But first we should head for Ulva. I know it's hard to believe, Muirne, but I'm convinced of it. We'll find the other three answer there in these three places. That's my theory anyway, Muirne. Decide! Do we go there or not?" Muirne carefully put the scroll away again.

"Ulva is miles away from here, Dom. There is also the small matter of water and lots of it between here and there. And we mustn't forget our friends the Golkani." They were both silent as reality hit them. They might just have begun to see that a map was in their possession that would lead them to the answers to the riddle, but they were still trapped. There was no way out. "Alright. We'll chance it. We'll go." But they both knew that was impossible without a miracle. Suddenly a soft rustling formed around them and the earth became a sheen of black feathers which rose up behind the standing stone to form a flying bridge. Not rats but ravens!

"Run, Dom, run across it as fast as you can," Muirne shouted, as she raced ahead of him yet again. Dom did not stop to question her order as the bridge of ravens flew beneath their feet and out over the water till the island of Ulva rose up from the azure depths below. Far away, the frantic scrabbling of the Golkani, taken unawares, reached them as the rushing, coolness of the air gave Dom and Muirne real hope that their quest might be successful after all.

chapter 8

The raven bridge seemed to climb higher and higher into the rays of the sun before suddenly plunging down as it flew over the wooded island sitting cool and dark in the blue-green marbled sea below. Muirne tried to close her ears to the furious, shrill protests of the Golkani as their quarry seemed to slip out of their grasp.

"Gorach!" shouted Dom above the heart-stopping din. Muirne gazed in fright as Gorach's mighty form loomed alongside. But as his hand tried to grab her, it was pecked by a dozen black ravens as the bridge suddenly disintegrated and Dom and Muirne fell to earth. The ravens continued to provide a protective covering as the soft branches of hazel trees gently lowered the two to earth. As the birds flew off, Muirne knew they were the ones she had released from the sacristy.

"Stay in the shelter of the woods," shouted Dom to Muirne as he zig-zagged his way through the dappled light and shade of the trees. "The Golkani need space to fly. We're safe here for a while."

The Golkani arrived screaming and diving but they were too late for Muirne and Dom were already entering the dense woods of Ulva upon their quest for the second answer to 'Tell me the secret.'

"Stop, Dom. We'll have to decide what we're going to do next. We need another answer." Muirne saw the sparkling waters of a lochan ahead and just over to their right, by the raised bank of a stream, an old thatched cottage. Maybe this was where they would discover the second piece of the puzzle. Dom saw it too and stood looking at it warily.

"Remember, Muirne, nothing is as it seems," he warned. That much he had learned from his short stay in this weird world.

"But we can't afford the time to examine every bit of what we come across. It's already early-afternoon and by sunset, all will be lost forever."

"We shouldn't rush this, Muirne." But Dom knew she was right.

"We can and we will. Now let's at least get nearer and see if anybody's at home." The cottage sat some five metres above the lochan and a short distance from where the water fell steeply down over some rocks and into a bubbling stream that tripped and stumbled noisily on its way to the open sea. Muirne and Dom stayed in the shelter of the hazel trees that enclosed the cottage on three sides. The silence around them said that Gorach and his horde had been chased off for the moment by the abbey ravens.

"What do you think?" whispered Dom, eyeing the cottage warily.

"Looks deserted," said Muirne softly.

"Maybe. But there are some nets down on the shoreline."

"A fisherman's cottage then?" Dom nodded at Muirne's suggested. But the nets looked torn and neglected just like the cottage.

"Well, Muirne, we're not going to learn anything just by staying here. Let's have another quick look at you father's plan.

"Why?" asked Muirne, but she carefully unrolled the plan anyway and propped it up against the nearest tree trunk.

"This is the Ulva one and I think we're here - right in the middle of the island from what I could see from up above. That cottage is very important to our quest. I'm absolutely certain of it." Muirne tucked the plan away again.

"I think we should have a look, Dom. You walk round to the left and I'll walk the other way. We'll meet up by the door. But be very careful and call out straight away if anybody or anything appears."

"Muirne, I'm." He was cut short by Muirne.

"If you say you're hungry once more!" she threatened, glowering at him.

"Well, I am. I can see from here there's a small campfire. Looks a bit rubbishy but there are still some cold ashes hemmed in by stones so it must at least be half-decent. Maybe we could cook." Again Muirne glared at him.

"Cook what? Berries? We've no time to go hunting and I don't eat dead meat anyway. You're probably no good at cooking either. As for me, I'm definitely not in the mood. If you want to roam the earth forever seeing but unseen, good luck. I don't and that deadline is more important to me than the rumblings of an empty stomach. So what's it to be? We examine the cottage for signs of life and maybe find the second line of the riddle or we find a deer and persuade it to commit suicide so that you can have a venison steak. Which do you prefer?"

Tell me the Secret

"All right, Muirne, when you put it like that, the cottage it is," Dom conceded grudgingly. "What's the plan?"

"As I said, you walk round that side, I'll walk round this side, we'll meet up at the door and swap information. Even if that door is partly open, stay out of the cottage until we - and I mean 'we' - think it's safe to enter."

There were no windows. One door facing the water was the only break in the very thick stone walls.

"Roof's in reasonable condition," said Muirne quietly when they met up again. "The place really seems to be deserted but we haven't been inside yet. Someone must be taking care of it. Did you see anyone, Dom?" Dom shook his head. "Any sign of anyone's belonging?" He shook his head again. "Neither did I." said Muirne finding the whole situation very strange. "I wonder who's been cooking over that fire? Couldn't have been that long ago or the wind would have scattered the ashes all over the place."

"Passing hunters? Fishermen?" Dom suggested. "And while talking of fish," he said, " there's a magnificent salmon lying quite dead on top of a rock at the water's edge. Fish only takes a minute or two to cook. If you give it a wash, I'll hunt around for flint and sticks or something to make fire. Learned how to do that from my dad. He showed me how to do it."

"How to, yes, but did it actually work?" asked Muirne.

"No. We went along to the chip-van," Dom confessed. "But it's alright, I think, to eat fish raw," he added. But he had just gone off the whole idea.

"Chip-van?" Muirne waited patiently.

"I'll explain later. It's a long story." The time and cultural differences were too many for Dom to deal with right then.

"Thank you for offering, Dom, but I'm quite used to lighting fires and boiling water. Why don't you bring the salmon here after you've washed it and I'll wrap it in some leaves and bake it. There are plenty of twigs lying around. Rub them together and we'll have fire in moments. I expect a short time cooking and eating might just help us to get our thinking straightened out. We can discuss it all while we eat."

"Want me to wait here until we've opened the door?" asked Dom. The whole cottage looked weird to him.

"You go on down to the water. I'll be careful and I can run like the wind when I have to. And I've got Anluann in this pouch, nasty little brute that he is. I'll soon waken him up if he's needed."

"Right, I'll be as quick as I can."

Dom hurried down the short distance to the rock below and leap onto it as the water lapped peacefully around. The salmon was of a good size and lay lifeless, its silver scales gleaming in the sun. Dom lifted it carefully and trailed it through the icy chill of the water. He heard Muirne's voice from above.

"This door is very stiff, Dom. Might just need your help after all. The two of us might just manage to open it between us."

"I'm coming. Finished here anyway. This salmon's a real beauty," he called up to her. He lifted the slippery fish and held it tightly as he began to climb up the slope to the flatter, grassy expanse in front of the old cottage.

"It's alright," called Muirne, " it's just jammed at the bottom. I'll give it a kick. Wait. That's strange." Dom heard her laugh. "It doesn't open inwards at all. It opens

Tell me the Secret

outwards. One big pull should do it." A sudden shrill, scream rent the air. "Dom! Quickly! Get out of the way!" Muirne shouted and Dom looked up as a cascade of slithering, jumping, leaping salmon poured forth frantically from the cottage and escaped back into the river. Dom never knew why he held onto the dead one. He just stood speechless, looking from Muirne to the joyful fish as they plunged and danced in the water on their way to freedom.

"Not so tightly, boy, not so tightly. I'm not going anywhere." Dom looked down at the dead salmon - only it was no longer dead but wriggling, annoyed in his arms. "And forget about cooking me. I'm nobody's fish course, understood? Tell the girl to come down here. I'll have a quick swim about while you do. Just to keep fit, you understand. Well, go on!" The very-much-alive salmon slid from Dom's arms and into the shimmering waters below before leaping once more onto what was obviously his favourite rock.

"Muirne! Come here! Fast!" But Muirne was already there staring oddly at the salmon. "This is one weird fish, Muirne," said Dom. "It can talk. I really don't think I can eat it." But Muirne had eased past him and was now seated on the rock beside the salmon.

"You know who I am, don't you," the salmon said to her. Muirne nodded.

"I do. You are Finlan, the Salmom of Wisdom. You gave all the knowledge of the world to Fionn mac Cumhaill." Dom was gob-smacked. Muirne did not seem to think that talking to a salmon was just a little bit bizarre.

"Without my family's help, Fionn would stand no chance against his great enemy, Mongann," said the salmon proudly.

"Quite so, Finlan. I am Muirne and this is Dom. But why were your brothers, the salmon, trapped in there?" Muirne asked. "That was a wicked and cruel thing to do. Who is responsible?" The magnificent salmon simply shook his head.

"The same one who always does it. We have lost so many of our people because of him."

"What's his name, Finlan? You must tell Fionn mac Cumhaill."

"Fionn's men have tried but Rochad is as slippery as an eel."

"So his name is Rochad?" said Muirne. Finlan, the salmon, nodded his head.

"Rochad the fisherman. Huge man with red hair and a beard to match. His wicked wife Eithlinn helps him. One is as bad as the other."

"But why catch so many? There are very few people living here. That is the first cottage Dom and I have seen. How can he trade them for other food and the goods he needs to live?"

"Because he is one of Mongann's men. Mongan buys them."

"I see," said Muirne thoughtfully. She turned to Dom and explained what it was all about as far as she knew. "Mongann is Fionn mac Cumhaill's sworn enemy."

"But what has all this to do with us, Muirne," said Dom aware that time was hurrying past. "We've no time to sit and swap stories about other-worldly heroes and villains."

"Why not?" asked the salmon angrily. "There's nothing other-worldly about it. This is the world you're living in.

Tell me the Secret

Get used to it. Mongann needs the salmon for their knowledge of the sea. No other sea-creature is as wise concerning nautical matters. The kelpies and silkies can say what they like, but it's true. All Mongann's warriors carry their battle equipment in their ships and, as they are so well-armed, they cannot have even the tiniest of oars on board or they will risk sinking the vessel." Muirne understood even if Dom did not.

"So the captive salmon are both their power and their navigators," she suggested to Finlan.

"Correct. Once harnessed to the ship like tugs, they cannot escape, only plough through the water till they die."

"That's outrageous," shouted Dom, "it shouldn't be allowed." Finlan smiled his thanks at this sympathy for their plight. "Rochad imprisons them inside huge tanks in that cottage until he has enough and then he sends for Mongann's men to come and fetch them from the lochan and take them as slaves. They will be here soon."

"That almost happened to me, Finlan," said Dom, " when this old woman." Muirne cut his story short.

"And what happens when they're too exhausted to be of any use?" she asked. But Finlan had already answered that in his own way.

"Where are Rochad and Eithlinn now?" asked Dom, horrified by what he had just heard and remembering how happy the salmon had been once they were free to swim and play. "They've gone to trap even more, I suppose?" he said. Finlan nodded and explained.

"There's a place where the salmon love to play. Near the place of the two waterfalls just to the north of here."

"Then we'll go there. Muirne and I will stop that evil pair. Take care, Finlan." Muirne turned to the salmon as they climbed back up the small incline.

"We'll do our best, I promise."

Dom followed as Muirne walked back to the cottage and peered in.

"Look," she said to Dom, " stone tanks where he kept them all crushed together. We must find that wicked pair." Dom nodded his agreement.

"Alright. Get the plan out and see what it tells us. I don't believe meeting Finlan was accidental. I'm sure it's all part of the quest. It was meant to happen, all part of our journey," he said.

"But we didn't get any answer that would fit into our riddle," Muirne reminded him, disappointed in a way she could not explain.

"But I didn't hear you actually ask him the question either, did I, Muirne?"

"You're right. I suppose I was hoping it would all just fall into our laps. Anyway, something told me that Finlan doesn't have the answer, that he wasn't the one who could tell us."

"Oh, that second sight again, I suppose," teased Dom. "Now, you deal in instinct, I deal in maps."

"Dom," said Muirne placing her father's plan before him, " Deoca was wicked and so is Rochad and Eithlinn according to Finlan. Maybe we can only get to the truth of it all by overcoming evil." Dom nodded knowingly.

"And that puts my mate Gorach right back in the frame. And, Muirne, that is a very nice bit of reasoning, but I'd be more impressed if you told me exactly how we're going to do it."

chapter 9

Dom nodded in agreement as Muirne spoke.
"It stands to reason that Rochad and Eithlinn will be further upriver," she said. "Salmon have their favourite haunts and this river seems to be one of them for the locals." Dom was puzzled as they made their way through the dense forest keeping the river in sight.
"How will they get their catch back? There seem to be no pathways where he could use a pony and cart to shift such a heavy load and he needs to keep them alive. It's all just forest tracks around here where there's hardly enough room for one person to walk never mind the width of a cart."
"I think, Dom, he'll not move away from the river bank. He'll be using a net like the old one back at the cottage. He'll catch them by stringing it across the narrowest part of the river and then haul them in. It's not a very wide stretch of water at all. He'll keep them in the water in the net all bunched up and healthy till he's ready to let the flow of the water take it back downstream to his cottage. He and Eithlinn will take the ropes and control the net as it goes. Quite simple really."
"Just walk it down?" said Dom.
"That's right. Hardly any effort required. Once back there, they'll probably tie it to Finlan's large rock, take the salmon

a bucketful at a time up to the storage tanks and then the net is free to be used again." Muirne stopped and listened. Only birdsong. They were in the forest among some ancient oaks but she still felt very wary about the Golkani. She walked on again as Dom spoke.

"He won't be happy to know the others are back in the river again, free and happy. Who'll tell him, Muirne, you or me?" They both laughed at the thought.

"Come on, Dom, we must hurry. Time seems to be rushing by and what if Rochad knows nothing about the secret?" Dom brushed that suggestion aside immediately.

"Of course he does!" But he was worried about that too.

They ran as fast as they could through the trees, hazel and gnarled oak of a great age, the dappled sunlight at times hurting their eyes and making them miss their step. Suddenly Dom's hand shot out and stopped Muirne from colliding with him as he halted and signalled Muirne to listen. The sounds ahead cheered them both up. Rochad and Eithlinn were only metres ahead. One man's voice, one woman answering him. It had to be them. Muirne smiled for the first time in hours, it seemed - until the air was rent by a chilling scream. Dom felt his breathing had stopped. Muirne dropped down, crouching as near to the leaf-strewn earth as possible. She hauled Dom down beside her as he seemed rooted to the spot. A Golkani scout! They could see its shadowed form as it searched the clearing ahead for them. They hardly dared to breathe. It darted about, rising and falling, forwards and back, moving at terrific speed and screaming furiously as if it knew for certain they were hiding close by. But they were still deep among the trees, their sprawling, twisted branches preventing anything or

Tell me the Secret

anyone having a clear view of the interior of the forest. There was no way it could either see them or reach into the wood. A few minutes later, all was silent among the foliage, only the distant screeching sounds fading quickly away as it sped off elsewhere, satisfied its quarry had not come that way. Dom rose very warily as he spoke.
"That was very scary, Muirne, I don't mind admitting that."
Muirne had no time to be scared.
"Move. We'll think about it later. We've got to question Rochad."
"And set the salmon free - if he's caught any," Dom reminded her. But Muirne needed no reminding.
"That too," she said brushing the debris of the forest floor from her skirt, " we'll make that the priority." She checked Anluann was still sound asleep.
"Everything alright?" asked Dom as he cleaned his dust-caked hands on his joggies. "You know, Muirne, these dead leaves really stink," he complained.
"They're just damp. The sun doesn't reach into this part but the rain does. You can scrub your hands in the river. Now, move." They hurried on and followed the course of the narrow river, careful to make as little noise as possible in the still air.

The sudden thrashing sound of the water ahead stopped them dead in their tracks. Muirne waited while Dom crawled on another few metres and peered down at the river bank. He then turned and nodded to Muirne. They had found the fisherman and he had found his new catch for it was stressed-out salmon, desperate to escape, that were making the thrashing sounds. But where was Eithlinn?

Tell me the Secret

"Where can she be?" whispered Muirne as she joined Dom and looked around. Dom shook his head as he watched Rochad haul in the net full of struggling salmon and then tie it off, hitching it over a huge rocky outcrop by the river bank. And this was certainly Rochad for there was no mistaking the height of the man with his red hair and beard.

"No idea," Dom replied quietly, "can't see her anywhere. He's working alone as far as I can see. But we heard her voice. She has to be here. What next?" They both moved back a little to where they definitely could not be seen. Muirne rested her back against an enormous tree trunk.

"Two things we must do," she said, "set the salmon free and talk to Rochad. He mustn't guess we've spoken to Finlan or released the trapped fish. We must make him think we've just happened upon them by chance."

"Collecting berries?" suggested Dom.

"Something like that. He must know nobody lives around here. We'll say we're on our way to work at Mongann's hunting lodge. If his boats come here to pick up the salmon, he's bound to have a place where they can hunt for food while they wait for Rochad to sort things out. Warriors don't see themselves as mere fishermen. That means they'll need kitchen staff for the great hall they're bound to have."

"And we'll say we're going to help. Brilliant, Muirne. Or maybe say we're travelling entertainers who sing, dance and throw in a bit of juggling. They might ask us to demonstrate. Can you sing, Muirne?"

"I've no idea for Mother forbade even humming."

"That was a bit harsh. Alright. I think we'll just bin that idea. We'll begin by getting as much information as we can

Tell me the Secret

out of Rochad before setting the salmon free. Is that the plan? Are you alright with that?" asked Dom.

"It is, for if we set the fish free first, Rochad will never stop to talk and we'll be running for our lives with absolutely no chance even to ask our question never mind hear the answer. Dom, let's begin with saying we've lost our way and ask him for direction's to Mongann's hall."

"Sounds reasonable. Then what, Muirne?" Muirne shook her head.

"I don't know."

"The problem as I see it is how to introduce the subject of the secret into the conversation? We can't just say, 'Listen, mate, you know the answer to the question- why do we call it a question, Muirne, for it's really a request?" Muirne's look told him to forget being accurate and just get on with it. Sorry - 'the question'Tell me the Secret', so let's have it.' He'll either think we're stupid or do something completely drastic without bothering to think at all. I've a rough idea that Rochad has a very imaginative mind which also doubles up as a very evil one." Muirne was not about to argue against that conclusion.

"Sounds drastic, Dom, but I think getting straight to the point is the only way to do it. I think Rochad has to be forced into just about everything he does. He's no deep thinker, more a reactor. My instincts all tell me he's the one with the answer we need. Without it, we can't move on. You make your way down to the nets and look a bit gormless as you go. He might be the kind of guy who hits out first and thinks later. Don't let him think you're any threat to him for he'll be watching you every step of the way."

"Fine, Muirne, but what will you do? Nothing silly, remember," he warned. Muirne gave him a look that made Dom wish he'd kept his mouth tight shut. She suddenly grinned at him. They were a team, she thought, and she would never complete the quest without his help.

"I'll go over to where he's sitting. He's obviously finished working for today. Maybe Eithlinn is cooking food somewhere." Dom shook his head.

"I don't smell wood smoke."

"Alright, maybe he loves berries and seeds and there are lots of hazelnuts lying around here, too," Muirne suggested watching Dom screw up his face. "Or maybe he just isn't hungry and Eithlinn's washing his hose. I don't know. All I do know is that we'd better get a move on or we'll have run out of time. If Rochad has the answer to our question, whatever way I put it to him, he's bound to know what I mean. Now, you get down there and, here, take Anluann with you. When you reach the net, and if you see I'm getting nowhere persuading him nicely to co-operate, call out and threaten to let Anluann loose. Seems as if everybody knows the power and temper of the dirk. But remember, whatever you do, don't waken him up unless the situation is desperate. Just say you'll make him burn through the massive ropes and release the salmon if he doesn't tell me the secret."

"So first we introduce ourselves," said Dom.

"Right. Then you go down to admire the salmon in the net, you being employed in Mongann's kitchen and an authority on fish dishes," said Muirne.

"And that's when you ask him the secret, Muirne?"

"Not the best way, I'll admit, but we haven't time for the social niceties. And if he doesn't tell me, you threaten him with our little friend, Anluann. Wave him about a bit but don't waken him up. Just so that Anluann thinks he's being rocked to sleep. But hold him tight," warned Muirne, "for we'll need him till this is all over."

"But how am I to rescue the salmon without Anluann's help? How can I free them from the net?" Dom could see endless problems. Muirne had not really thought this through but he supposed time was the main factor in it all. They had to improvise, make decisions on the spot with very little information available to them. It was a miracle they had managed to get this far and still be in one piece.

"Rochad's knife is on the rock beside him. I'll grab it and throw it down to you. You can use it to cut the net."

"And then, Muirne, we just walk away as soon as he answers the question. Tell me the secret or else, you say. Certainly, madam, he says. Then he tells you and we just saunter away. Reality check here, Muirne. If he knows the secret, he won't let us just walk away once he's been forced into revealing it," warned Dom.

"How right you are!" The arrow zipped past their heads as Eithlinn released it before quickly replacing it with another in her bow. This one was aimed directly at Muirne's heart. "Rochad! We've got company!"

chapter 10

Rochad's eyes bore right through Dom, green as emeralds, hard as flint. Eithlinn's arrow remained pointing straight at Muirne.

"Who are they?" asked Rochad.

"Said they're going to Mongann's hunting lodge to work in the kitchens." Eithlinn found that very funny. How much else had she heard? Dom wondered.

"Like we said," blustered Dom, "we're nobody really, just kitchen help for the great Mongann. Is he your master too? Are those salmon for a feast? Is that why he needs extra help like us?" He was twittering and he knew it but Dom just could not help himself.

"The boy's a fool," laughed Eithlinn and Rochad sniggered as he stopped close by. It was a wholly, evil sound. Dom's blood felt as if it had frozen in his veins. Right then, he did not think there was much to choose between Rochad and Gorach for wickedness. Muirne said nothing. She might at least have stuck up for him, thought Dom, giving her a resentful glare. But maybe she was just too scared to speak, maybe it was all up to Dom now.

"All right," he said, " we're not going to Mongann's to help out. We're pick-pockets and we've heard there are rich pickings to be had there as Mongann is so wealthy and gives his loyal followers great rewards."

Tell me the Secret

"First we've heard of that," said Rochad sceptically. Dom ignored that comment and carried on.

"We just want a little of it to take back home. We live on the shores of Loch na Lathaich. Lots of coracles and boats come into the shore to buy supplies. We could trade for what we need if we can steal a few worthwhile things like spoons and bowls and maybe some dried berries." Dom finally stuttered to a halt. He knew when he was wasting his time. "Please just lower that arrow," he pleaded quietly.

"Quite finished?" asked Rochad sarcastically. "Finally run out of rubbish?" Dom thought he saw a slight smile flit across Muirne's face. Some friend. He would never have let anyone talk to her like that. Then again, the arrow was not pointing straight at his heart. "Maybe they really are just two hopeless thieves, Eithlinn. We could just tie them to the rocks in the river before we leave and let the flash flood that's now overdue, take care of them. That heavy rain on the very dry ground has always spelled trouble before. There's only one result, isn't there?" Eithlinn nodded wisely and seemed positively cheered up by the very thought.

"What a splendid idea, Rochad. You're just full of them, aren't you. An odd one but a good one nonetheless. Never fails. Fancy a bit of venison for your supper later on?" Rochad nodded and looked delighted at the prospect.

"With some rowan berry jelly?" he suggested.

"Absolutely. Now, have we got any spare rope?" she asked and Rochad quickly put her mind at ease.

"We'll truss them up in the spare net like we do the salmon. They can remain here and we can get on with taking the salmon back to the cottage."

"A very neat solution, Rochad," said Eithlinn in admiration.
"Dom," whispered Muirne.
"Shut up!" screamed Eithlinn, "say nothing. Not a single sound will come from your mouth or I'll lose this arrow." Rochad shook his head.
"Just loose it if you like, Eithlinn. We've got to be going. Mongann's men will be here shortly and we have much to do back at the cottage. Let her speak to the boy. No doubt she'll tell him how pathetic he sounds. You," he said pointing to Dom, " start moving and remember the arrow's direction can be changed in an instant."
"Leave him, Rochad, the boy is nobody. He's no danger to us." Dom looked at Muirne who had been watching Eithlinn intently all the time. He knew that they were both wondering the same thing. Why had Eithlinn singled out Muirne? Why had she panicked when Muirne had begun to speak? There was fear in Eithlinn's eyes yet she was the one with the weapon. Dom felt some of that fear in his own stomach. Fear made people do crazy things and Eithlinn's fear could get Muirne killed. But what could they do when they didn't know what was causing it? He felt that if he ran for it to try and draw Eithlinn's attention away from Muirne, that just would not happen. Somehow Muirne was the one who mattered to Eithlinn, not Dom. He was convinced that Rochad, too, had no idea what it was all about. Two people had blundered into his operation and had to be silenced. As far as Rochad was concerned, that was all it was. A bit of inconvenience that could easily be taken care of. Rochad's thick, deep voice slithered its way through the silence.
"Who is she? What is she, Eithlinn?" So Rochad was no fool after all.

Tell me the Secret

"She is Mariota!" Everything stopped. No bird-song, no sound of rushing water, no breeze sighing through the trees. Then Gorach rose up from the river and instantly Dom threw Anluann at him, caught him a glancing blow and Gorach vanished cursing furiously.

"The salmon! They're escaping! It's scorched holes in the net!" called Rochad and rushed down to save his smouldering net and its catch. Dom rushed down headlong behind him. Anluann was still dazed by the sudden awakening and Dom had him back in his pouch before he recovered.

"She's not Mariota," shouted Dom, " she's Muirne and we want to know the secret." Muirne still said nothing for her mind was reaching far back into the past - her own past. That was where the answers lay. Mariota had said they had all that they needed with them to solve it, so what was it that Eithlinn was so afraid of? Why had she mistaken Muirne for Mariota? Or did she, Muirne, have a power that had once belonged to the mysterious Mariota? And if so, what was it and how had Muirne come to possess it?

"Tell them nothing Rochad. That was a secret between you and me." Eithlinn's eyes darted momentarily from Muirne to Rochad as she shouted to him.

"I gave you my word, Eithlinn, and I won't break it." Eithlinn laughed in triumph.

"Then you two are wasting your time. Go! Both of you," she cried, " before I change my mind and let Rochad have his way with your fate." She turned once more to Muirne. "You remain silent. This arrow will be aimed at you until we can see you no more." But Dom had other ideas.

"Not before we learn the answer to our question. The secret. Tell us what it is?" he shouted as Rochad grabbed him hauled him up the bank by his hoodie. At the top, Rochad shook him violently till Dom felt his brains must be rattling about loose in his skull. But the shaking stopped suddenly as the beautiful, lilting notes of sweet singing filled the still, warm air.

"I warned you to shut up!" Eithlinn screamed at Muirne. But it was too late and Eithlinn knew it. Rochad was enthralled, held spellbound by Muirne's singing. "Don't listen to her," she pleaded, "close your ears to it, Rochad." Rochad had let Dom go and was now walking slowly, as if in a trance, towards Muirne. Dom saw the anger rise in Eithlinn.

"That arrow! Put it down!" he shouted as Muirne continued to sing. Dom raced towards Eithlinn and knocked the bow out of her hands.

"She is Mariota, Rochad," insisted Eithlinn, sobbing. "She's come to lure you away from me."

"As if," said Dom, " and who'd want him?" Muirne quickly signalled to Dom to keep his opinions to himself.

"We need him, Dom," she whispered as her intoxicating sounds lingered in the air. "He's the way forward for us. This is the only way to discover the secret." Eithlinn's sharp ears heard her.

"Rochad only knows part of it. You're wasting your time and your singing has no effect on me. You're beaten. Leave right now," Eithlinn ordered. But Muirne continued to sing, luring Rochad away from Eithlinn. Dom could not believe what was happening. The evil Rochad was mesmerised by Muirne's singing. Was this why her mother had never allowed Muirne to sing? Had she known of the power that voice held? How it seemed to be able to control real wickedness? Was Muirne really Mariota? Dom swallowed hard and tried to keep his nerve in a situation he did not understand. He wanted out of there, wanted away from magic and legends and power that could be used for either good or evil in the twinkling of an eye. He could run. Eithlinn had ordered them to go and she still had that bow and the arrows. It would mean escaping Rochad, the truly evil one, and Gorach, the complete nutcase. He did not think for one moment they were fans of his.

"Muirne," he said, "Gorach will be back. We must go."

"Not before she tells us the secret." Muirne turned to Eithlinn. "Rochad is coming with us." The sweet notes still filled the air as the sounds seem to echo from the rocky outcrops above the river. "We must leave. Now." She turned away towards Dom and Rochad meekly followed. Eithlinn suddenly cried out,

"No! Don't take him! He's my husband. How else will I earn food and have shelter from the harsh days of winter if I'm all alone?" Muirne ignored her plea.

"Come Dom, Rochad."

"No! All right. I'll tell you what you want to know." Muirne and Dom waited until Eithlinn forced herself to tell the secret. "It's 'I am nothing'. Now will you go and leave Rochad and me in peace?" she cried. Dom groaned. Another bit of information that made no sense. "Now release Rochad from your spell, Mariota." Muirne nodded. "He'll sleep for a while but remember, Eithlinn, a spell once lifted can be put on again."

Tell me the Secret

As they entered the forest once more, Muirne turned back and called to Eithlinn,

"And I'm definitely not Mariota!"

"Then how do you have her voice, her power?" cried Eithlinn. Muirne felt Dom's hand grab her arm and drag her into the shade of the ancient oaks and away from the hateful look on Eithlinn's face.

"Just ignore her," he said. But he knew that was easier said than done - for both of them. "We'll stop in the first clearing and discuss what to do next. Did that part of the puzzle make any sense to you, Muirne," asked Dom.

"None," was Muirne's short and simple answer.

"How did you know to sing to him?" said Dom.

"I just heard myself do it. I don't know why"

"Well, it certainly worked. I wonder if your mother knew that you had that power. Was that why she didn't let you sing?"

"I've no idea and we don't have the time to work it out." Dom could tell by the sharp tones that Muirne was shaken by what was happening to her.

"You're right, Muirne. Move on. That's the best idea but you might as well have this. It's a pebble belonging to Rochad. He dropped it when he grabbed me and I picked it up. He was desperate to get it back but I had Anluann and he hadn't. No contest. Could be our second object."

They travelled silently for a short time then stopped when they reached a small glade and the light was enough to see by. Neither mentioned again the strange power Muirne's voice had held and Muirne being mistaken for Mariota. There was some kind of bond there but what was it? The unspoken question hung in the air between them.

Tell me the Secret

"Right, let's have another look at your father's plan. What did Eitlinn say? 'I am nothing.' So we have that and 'I begin at the end'. Great!"

"We need the rest of it, Dom, to make sense of it all," said Muirne carefully unrolling the little bit of parchment. Dom studied it intently before shaking his head.

"So where to next? And as you're the one with the magical powers, Muirne, you tell me," teased Dom.

"That's not funny. I think Rochad was suffering from a bit of sunstroke. It's very hot and, remember, he's been catching fish in the sun all day. It was probably just a coincidence and one that worked to our advantage. Maybe the rowan jelly he likes so much was off." Muirne shrugged. Dom finally asked the question Muirne was dreading.

"What about the Mariota angle? That wasn't Rochad, that was Eithlinn and she sounded very sane to me."

"Maybe they're both addicted to rowan jelly," Muirne suggested trying to shrug the whole thing off. "But I agree that Eithlinn knew straight away what we were talking about. That had nothing to do with Rochad. That only helped her make up her mind to tell us. Anyway, that part is behind us. Where to next?" The subject of Mariota was closed and Dom knew it.

"Well," he said, peering closely at the plan, "this is hard for nothing really jumps out as our next destination. Another island, probably, but which one?" He tried hard to bring the images of the pages of his school atlas to mind. "I'm puzzled by all these sort of triangles and shapes in this long rectangle. Shapes! That's it - maybe."

"Dom, decide fast, very fast," said Muirne grabbing the plan and quickly putting it away as she backed into the forest once more. "Look!"

"Gorach!" Dom had scarcely uttered that chilling name before the air was filled with the screeching and howling of the demented Golkani. "Run, Muirne, run for your life. We have to get to Staffa." But how?

chapter 11

They fled. Fear made their feet take wings. They could hear the clash of the metal, nail extensions, the whirring of the quartered-coloured eyes.

"There's nowhere to run to, Dom," cried Muirne. Dom knew that only too well. They could not break cover but the trees were becoming more sparse and that meant the Golkani would be able to pick them off at will.

"Just keep going!" he yelled back. There was nothing else they could do. The sea suddenly loomed up before them and both Dom and Muirne stopped abruptly.

"Keep on coming! We're here to help you!" a voice called out to them. Finlan! "Come on! Quick!" But the air between Finlan and the forest was suddenly thick with swooping, screeching Golkani, their ferocious talon-like nails with the swinging metal tips clashing as they went.

"We hear you, Finlan," cried Muirne.

"We'll never make it across open ground," yelled Dom and wondered how the great salmon could possible save them.

"You'll have to. There is no other way and the sun is beginning to go down. You must hurry. You must leave the shelter of the trees." Muirne and Dom backed away until they found a spot where the trees were more dense and a barrier to the Golkani. Muirne sat down on a tree trunk as Dom squatted down among the fallen leaves.

"Finlan's right, Dom. We have to try to reach the shore although I don't see that that will be any better than here," she said.

"Unless there's a boat tied up there," suggested Dom. They looked at each other and the memories of their last trip in that other boat from Iona came flooding painfully back. Still, it would be their only hope.

"What could Finlan possibly do to save us?" Muirne asked. But Dom could only shrug his shoulders.

"The answer to that must surely be 'nothing', Muirne. "He's probably just not thought it through, just very anxious to help us." The screaming and screeching continued above the trees and between Dom, Muirne and the shimmering azure and emerald-tinted line ahead that marked the horizon.

"Maybe if I climbed a tree I could see if Finlan had a boat, Dom," suggested Muirne. Dom pulled a face.

"Just hope it's not a crystal one!" he said sourly. "But that won't work either - climbing a tree, I mean - for the minute you poke your head out of the branches, the Golkani will be down on you."

"I suppose you're right." Dom got up suddenly and sat on the log beside Muirne.

"Have you thought of something?" she asked eagerly.

"Well, a bit of an idea. We can talk it over and see if we think it's workable."
"What is it?" asked Muirne, anxious to be well clear of Ulva. The idea had sounded good to Dom when it had first occurred to him but would it still be so when voiced aloud to Muirne? She would surely see any drawbacks in it immediately. Dom cleared his throat and began.
"We have to get from the tree-line to the water without being caught by Gorach and his vicious little mates, the Golkani."
"That much has been obvious for quite some time, Dom," said Muirne scathingly.
"Agreed. We therefore have to find a way to cross the open ground without being seen or at least without the Golkani touching us."
"Don't even begin to mention singing and Mariota, Dom, or, so help me, I'll get to you before the Golkani and you might just wish they'd got to you first." Dom avoided looking at her and began to untie his trainers and remove the laces.
"Could you empty two of your pouches into one, Muirne?" he asked her.
"I could. But why?"
"I need the pouches." The leather was soft and thick. "Would you do it now, please. The sun won't wait for us you know." Muirne looked slightly annoyed at this comment reminding her of the sunset deadline but did as he asked. "Just trust me."
"All yours," she said and handed him the empty pouches then watched in amazement as he slipped his feet into them, tying them in place with the vibrant, yellow laces he had

taken from his trainers. "Bit bright," was all Muirne said as she watched this performance.

"That's rich coming from someone who thinks creatures with purple scaly skin and four-coloured eyes are normal."

"Of course they're normal. In their country, they all look like that. You'll have to learn to widen your horizons, be more open to new ideas. Now get a move on and explain." Dom took the hint.

"There's no way we can avoid the Golkani once we're out in that open space so I think that we might have a go at crossing the space unnoticed."

"Make ourselves invisible?" asked Muirne. Dom nodded seriously. "Now why didn't I think of that?" Muirne shook her head in exasperation. Dom ignored her.

"That's right, invisible," he said. "Well, in a sort of way. We'll be there, running very quietly, but they just won't see us."

"Do you have a spell you've been hiding from me?" Muirne's look said it was simply not going to happen.

"Nope. No magic at all, only common sense, Anluann and my trainers - shoes to you," he added.

"I'm listening." Muirne thought she might as well hear Dom out for she herself had no ideas at all that would solve the problem.

"These trainers will burn and, as they're partly made of a material called rubber, they'll cause a great deal of smoke. I thought that we could steal down to the water's edge under cover of the smoke. It would make us invisible to the Golkani. They won't be able to see us and their eyes will sting so much they'll back off."

"What about our eyes?" asked Muirne.

"Good question," said Dom. "We'll just have to keep them covered as much as possible and run like the wind. It should only take a few moments to cover the ground if we don't have to fight off the Golkani. All we have to do is waken Anluann and have him burn the rubber in both trainers for maximum effect, making sure that we hang onto him like grim death. We don't want to lose him and we certainly don't want Gorach to get him back."

"And once he's completed his task?" asked Muirne.

"Anluann goes back to his water-bed. You can grind him some herbs as a treat. Use Rochad's pebble. I hope it was his lucky talisman and he's gutted to have lost it. Back to business. I'll throw the trainers right out into the open space between us and the water where the wind will whip up the smoke and off we go. That's it." Dom sighed into the never-ending silence that followed and shrugged. "Just thought it worth a try."

"Well done, Dom. Let's do it!"

Anluann was not happy to have his dream disturbed. But he enjoyed burning holes in Dom's trainers and then he went contentedly back to bed and what he thought was a well-earned rest.

"It's working, Muirne," whispered Dom as they waited until the breeze fanned the smouldering trainers into a huge cloud of dense, black smoke. The Golkani backed off rapidly, confused and spluttering.

"Now, Dom, run!" urged Muirne.

"Just hope Finlan has everything in hand.," he whispered back.

They ran, bent low, as soundlessly as they could. They raced straight ahead and hoped they were not running into very deep water.

"This way!" called Finlan. The whispered order gave then a direction to aim for and hope soared within them. Did Finlan have a boat after all? Muirne and Dom felt the ground beneath their feet change from woodland crunch to a soft, slippery surface and the air suddenly cleared.

"Staffa, Finlan, that's where we must go," Dom called to the salmon. They were moving rapidly along, closed within some kind of glistening container, it seemed. They both fell on their knees and took deep gulps of air while blinking furiously to clear the smoke from their eyes which had nipped and stung as they has passed through it.

"Where are we?" asked Muirne. She looked at Finlan as he smiled on both his friends. "What are we in?" she asked him, puzzled. She could hear the rushing sound of the sea outside as the vessel they were in rose and dived and rolled a little.

"You are both safe and on your way to Staffa. My salmon friends have simply formed a sort of guard of honour around you and we are now all skimming our way through the waves to Staffa. I did hear correctly? It was where you wanted to go, wasn't it?" asked Finlan anxiously, looking from Dom to Muirne. Dom nodded and smiled in amazement.

"You mean the salmon have formed a kind of boat around us?" he asked in astonishment. Finlan smiled with relief.

"Well, one good turn deserves another. You helped them and now it's their chance to help you."

"So," said Muirne, "we are really inside a sort of giant salmon whose shape is made up of all the ones that were in Rochad's nets, Finlan?"

"Absolutely. Fun, isn't it? They are swimming together so closely that this inside space is water-tight. We'll have reached Staffa in no time at all and I understand how precious time is for both of you, Muirne. Right now, the Golkani will still be trying to stop their whirring eyes stinging. Pity about your shoes though, Dom. Was that what you used to create smoke? Anluann doing what he does best?" Dom nodded. They all looked at Dom's feet wrapped tightly in their leather pouches tied fast with the laces. "Can't be helped, though," said Finlan briskly. "Besides, you've still got the laces. A bit bright, aren't they?" Dom kept his mouth tight shut - with difficulty. A person could definitely go off fish, he thought.

"We're very grateful, Finlan, for all your help," said Muirne quickly, "aren't we Dom."

"Very grateful, Finlan," he agreed and meant it. He could always get another pair of trainers if and when he returned to the 21st century. Finlan had begun talking again and Dom and Muirne listened intently.

"When we reach Staffa, the boys here will drop you off in the main cave and then turn and dive and make their way back out to the open water again. All in one smooth movement," Finlan added proudly. "It's a bit of a tricky manoeuvre as the space is very confined and we are so many, but not an insurmountable problem to salmon. Ingenuity is a salmon's middle name. But the two of you must be very careful on the ledges for the sea sweeps in and crashes over the lower ones all the time," warned Finlan.

"You mean they're very wet and slippery," said Muirne.
"Yes. Wait a second, can you feel us slowing down?" Muirne and Dom both nodded and felt the excitement rising within. "Be ready to jump as the salmon part." They waited, hardly daring to breathe. "Now!" Finlan shouted. The space around them opened and the thundering sound of the waves crashing against the massive, hexagonal pillars almost deafened Muirne and Dom.
"Jump onto the ledge," cried Muirne to Dom as their salmon sanctuary vanished down beneath the foaming brine. They were slammed hard against the jagged, slippery wall of the enormous, cathedral-like cavern. Staffa! Did the third solution lie here?

chapteR 12

The hexagonal basalt columns soared high above them and Muirne and Dom were stunned by their incredible beauty. Deep inside the cave, whose floor was the thundering, crashing foam-topped sea, its far wall glistened a sparkling rosy pink hue as wave after wave bounced back off it.
"These slabs of rock are dangerous. Finlan was right," Dom shouted above the roar of the emerald-green streaked sea. "We'd be better trying to back out and climb up to the top of the island." Muirne nodded. "It's too dangerous in here," he said.

"If we tumble off, there's no help so be very careful," Muirne warned as they edged back nervously along the cave and out onto the rocky surface of Staffa. It was like nothing Dom had ever seen or even heard of. Nothing there except the individual flat slabs. No two columns, some no size at all, others soaring majestically, were the same height. It was a scene of two planets having collided and left behind an incredible one of a terrible beauty. Dom was speechless. It was truly awesome. There was no gentle earth beneath their feet, just hard treacherous terrain that could spell disaster from broken bones or from being pitched into the depths of the Sound of Iona. How on earth could this be the place where their next clue lay? thought Muirne.

"I'm soaked through," shouted Dom above the crashing waves as the sea ebbed and flowed in a foam-filled frenzy forcing spray sky-high. Muirne and Dom finally made it to some low columns just out of reach of the icy water and both slumped down, soaked to the skin. Muirne looked at Dom and got her word in first.

"You're drenched and hungry, I know," she said, now able to speak instead of shouting. "I think we've had this conversation before."

"You can add and 'out of ideas' to that," said Dom shivering. Muirne understood. The island did look as if there was absolutely nothing to be learned there as far as their quest was concerned. She felt deeply disappointed as Dom spoke again. "This place is definitely incredible, though. That part over there looks like a giant has been playing a game of dominoes with hexagonal pieces, lost the game and knocked the whole lot over in a huff."

Tell me the Secret

"Don't think I know that game," said Muirne thoughtfully. "But, of course, there's no reason to suppose we're not dealing with giants. A giant would count as one very ordinary person in the world we're now in," Muirne reminded him. "But to get back to the reason we're here, it looks like you and I are marooned. Stuck! Here on this rocky nightmare." But Dom interrupted her quickly.

"I think it's stunningly beautiful, Muirne. An hexagonal-buff's wildest dream." She ignored him.

"The only people we can ask about the secret is ourselves. There's just these incredible columns and us here. That's it. A deserted, spectacular vision of fantastic shapes and nothing else."

"That's what you might think, Muirne," said Dom standing up quickly, "for, oddly enough, we have visitors. Better go and put the kettle on."

"What? Have you gone mad?" Muirne looked behind her in time to see several boats pull into what could be a landing place farther along the treacherous shore. Men hurried down from the flat rocky top of the cliffs above them and suddenly, it seemed Staffa was full to bursting point with people.

"Move yourselves," thundered a voice, "and help carry the firewood as it's unloaded unless you want to freeze to death tonight."

"It's alright, Diarmaid,. They've probably come to help with the food for Fionn's feast tonight. Edain wants them to help her." Muirne was thrilled there was someone to ask and maybe to answer the question of the secret. Dom was pleased to know that something to eat might be his very soon. But reality kicked in and he focused once more on the information they desperately needed. Yet again, though, they had no idea who could tell them the secret. "I'm Conall." Muirne looked closely at the boy. He was perhaps just a few years older than they were, about fourteen, she thought. That was good for grown-ups seldom listened to children and she and Dom definitely needed someone to listen to them. The one shouting the orders did not look like he would take time out to hear their story.

"I'm Muirne," she said, " and this is Dom." This Conall would not know the answer they were wanting to hear but he was obviously friends with the others and seemed to know what was going on.

"Have you just arrived? You look lost. Never been involved in one of these before?" asked Conall. Dom and Muirne both nodded.

"Looks very busy," ventured Dom. That's putting it mildly, he thought. The place was going like a fair. Maybe they were just all a bit too busy to listen, he thought, and that would have the same result as an island without anyone on it.

"People are coming from all over the land for the peace meeting between Fionn and the other chiefs and, of course, expecting a great feast afterwards. That's where you two come in. That's if Fionn doesn't lose his temper and storm off. Could be very dangerous round here if that happens," said Conall. "You see, none of them really get on with each other."

"Is he as bit touchy?" asked Dom. Fionn who? he thought. Then it suddenly dawned on him. "Are we talking about the great hero Fionn mac Cumhaill?" Who didn't know the legend of one of the greatest Celtic heroes of all time? "We

Tell me the Secret

really are talking about Fionn mac Cumhaill, Conall?" he asked again. Had Mariota really said he was her father? Mind you, he did remember reading that the bold Fionn had rather a lot of children dotted around. Dom glanced at Muirne but her deliberately blank expression gave nothing away.

"Who else? Who did you think has arranged all this? Of course, you're thinking of Mongann. Yes, he actually was top dog for a bit when Fionn was away in Ulster. But the big man's back now and don't we all know it. Have you two been away in the southlands for a while? Still to catch up with the political roundabout?"

"That's about it," said Muirne. "Is Mongann expected then?"

"Yes," said Conall, "he'll be here shortly. When all the chiefs and heroes have arrived, the peace treaty meeting will begin, everyone will huff and puff, nothing will been settled but they'll all pretend that it has, and then the feast to celebrate nothing in particular will begin. That's where we come in. The food and entertainment. There's nothing that truly great heroes love as much as a good fight as enjoying an equally good meal. The pact will last only as long as the food, they'll fall out again, hurl a few very telling insults at each other, then they'll all sail off and we'll begin all over again on another island. There are plenty of islands in these parts as you can see. I'm told Manannan mac Lir has already decided to bypass Staffa and just head on down south to Islay and book the best campsite for his followers. Finlaggan's a favourite spot. Rumour has it Islay is the next island on the meeting-place list. Should pass at any time now. It will be quite a spectacle if past experience is anything to go by."

"Likes to put on a good show, does he?" asked Dom fascinated.

"Manannan mac Lir is the son of the Sea God. Very theatrical turn of mind."

"Bit of a show-off," Dom suggested.

"You could say that, Dom, but not when he's about," advised Conall, smiling. Muirne was of a more serious and philosophical turn of mind.

"Still, I suppose when the great and the good are talking, they're not fighting," she said. Conall shook his head.

"Not so, Muirne, for I have personally seen them do both at the same time. Mongann can actually go one better than Fionn in this for he can shout, fight and eat all at the same time. Granted that when he does all three, he invariably loses the fight and those sitting close by tend to get food all over them. But the fact remains, he can actually do it."

"Badly," said Dom.

"Yes," agreed Conall and both boys found something heroic in the fact that Mongann tried to be different from the herd. Muirne reckoned all three of them were fools. "But Fionn is too busy tearing around fighting with everyone who might not keep the peace to keep the peace himself, so a really big battle is avoided," said Conall.

"Just really big feasts take place," asked Dom.

"Exactly." Muirne thought it was time to get moving and find out just how useful Conall could be in their search.

"Are you a kitchen boy?" she asked him. Conall nodded and was about to speak when Dom got his word in first.

Tell me the Secret

"Do you actually prepare the food? You see, Conall, I'm very hungry and I was wondering if you could see your way to giving us a bite to eat." Dom sounded pathetic. He could see that from the look on Muirne's face. But all Dom's hopes were dashed when Conall shook his head.

"I'm one of the great Fionn's bards. I'm a story-teller, a keeper of our people's history and traditions. We don't write anything down, just memorise the lot and sing them out at the great feasts. I play the harp as well, by the way," he said proudly, pointing to the instrument slung over his shoulder.

"A very important person then," said Muirne, impressed.

"Not as yet, Muirne. I'm about eleventh in the pecking order. Still learning the trade and, actually, I'm expected to help serve the food in my spare time with a bit of light cleaning thrown in when necessary."

"Hard luck, mate," said Dom with feeling as 'cleaning' was a word that he had no intention of allowing into his vocabulary. "Does all that boil down to a small snack being off the menu?" he added.

"Pardon?" said Conall.

"He means, Conall, are you unable to get him something to eat?"

"Oh, that's no problem. Come on. Hope you've got a head for heights, both of you."

Fionn mac Cumhaill towered over everyone and was in a foul mood.

"I don't know what his problem is," whispered Conall sticking to the most distant campfire from the hero. The land about, harsh and fragmented dips , rocky slopes and heights, bore few signs of springtime. Moss and stunted, coarse heather clung for dear life to the black, basalt hexagons. Dom was fascinated by those shapes that seemed to bear witness to the struggles of the planet at the very beginning of time itself.

"Don't stare at him! Don't attract Fionn's attention! Don't upset him!" whispered Muirne crouching down behind a broken column for some protection from the howling wind. All the oceans and storms of the world seemed to meet here. "Eat," ordered Muirne, "and then there's work to be done, questions to be asked."

"Then Fionn's your man," said Conall, the part-time bard and harpist. "One bite on his thumb and he sees the secrets of the world, all its wisdom is revealed to him."

"Really? Are you having us on?" asked Dom with his mouth still full of something that looked like a Big Mac but tasted like a liquorice and cardboard burger. Dom surprised himself by taking another one of the foul concoctions offered by Conall. Hunger made a boy do strange things. Muirne politely refused.

"Thanks, mate," he said. "Anything to drink?"

"Only mead, I'm afraid," said Conall.

"Mead?" Muirne quickly explained to Dom.

"Do you like honey?" she asked him.

"Hate it."

"Then you won't like mead."

"Any water then?" Conall shook his head.

"Not enough water on Staffa to go round. There's only a small spring and it's really hardly more than a trickle. We bring in our own supplies of mead. It's very popular."

Dom could understand that for there seemed to be hundreds

Tell me the Secret

of Fionn's warriors and their helpers swarming all over the place.

"Have some of the chiefs arrived?" he asked.

"Most of them. A great many are over on the other side of the island." Conall lifted his harp and began to tune it. "The salt water plays havoc with this," he complained.

"So who are they waiting for?" It seemed to Dom that everything was ready for the meeting.

"Mainly Mongann. It seems his ships have been held up due to unforeseen circumstances. Some hitch or other to their supply chain in Ulva." Muirne kept her eyes firmly on what she hoped was eggy bread. But what were those little black, striped bits in it? she wondered and wished she hadn't looked so closely. Dom suddenly downed the beaker of mead and immediately felt slightly woozy. The feeling soon passed, though, as the harsh wind whipped his face back to reality again.

"But why is everybody rushing about?" asked Muirne, for very few were sitting down and eating despite all the cooking pots reduced to simmering over the fires.

"We are about to be told just that. Shh! Listen!" Conall said quietly. A voice boomed out and the very upright columns of Staffa seemed to shake and the sea ceased its eternal singing in the great caverns. Fionn mac Cumhaill glared about him.

"My wand of office as leader if the Fianna!" he cried out to the four winds. "It's lost! Find it!" This greatest of warriors, fair of face and hair, looked threateningly round his followers.

"Without it, he'll lose face in front of Mongann and the others," whispered Conall. All was quiet except for the low moaning of the wind which seemed to echo the great warrior's mood. Fionn glowered some more and then spoke again.

"Whoever brings it to me, shall ask one question and he shall receive the answer from my great gift of knowledge that I received from Fintan the Salmon." Everyone knew that the right question could bring them untold wealth. There would be no shortage of searchers. Dom moved nearer Conall.

"Fionn means Finlan, doesn't he?" Dom asked, curious that the great man had slipped up there. Must really be rattled, he thought. Conall shook his head and replied in hushed tones.

"No, Fintan. Finlan is Fintan's nephew. Very smart family. But, Dom, listen carefully to Fionn mac Cumhaill." There really was no need to say that for both Dom and Muirne had realised what Fionn's offer could mean to them.

"Find it, Dom. We must," said Muirne quietly. "This is our one chance, and we must take it." Bran, Fionn's huge wolfhound leapt about his master's legs and Fionn understood its message. He bellowed out one more time before everyone scattered to find the wand.

"Mongann is now on his way here. Bran has sensed it. I must have that wand of office or that unworthy villain will have the say of life or death over all of us. Go! Search! Find it!" Fionn mac Cumhaill's voice faded as the frenzied roar of the waves boomeranged into the depths of the cathedral-like caves and filled the air with its voice once more.

Tell me the Secret

"It's alright saying 'Look!' but where do we start, Muirne?" asked Dom. Conall had already disappeared so there was no help from him.

"We must do this systematically, Dom," decreed Muirne.

""But that's impossible. We don't know where or when Fionn last had it." Dom was beginning to feel edgy. They were getting nowhere fast.

"Well, the 'where' must be on Staffa and the when doesn't matter This is almost hopeless." Dom suddenly stood up, grinning like a cat that had got at the cream.

"Oh no it isn't," he shouted as he ran off.

"What is it, Dom?" called Muirne as she followed him to the piece of land above a little rocky bay where the hexagonal shapes leaned almost flat as if the result of some great upheaval when the land was young. He stopped and laughed.

"Muirne, do you think dogs like to hide wands of office as well as bones?"

chapter 13

"Did Conall mention Gorach?" he asked Muirne.

"No." Muirne sounded very positive.

"Well, I'm sure I heard someone say it," said Dom frowning.

"It definitely wasn't Conall for I was listening very carefully to him. He's our only real source of information on Staffa and our only hope." Muirne sounded very positive about that too. "You probably heard one of the warriors mention it as he passed by. They're crashing about all over the place. No plan, no trying to reason it out. Dom, you're just fired up and scared."

"I am not!" protested Dom loudly, glaring at Muirne.

"Well, you should be. I certainly am. If that Mongann turns up with Rochad in the pack, we will certainly be in the soup."

"You can sing to him," suggested Dom, "that'll keep him quiet."

"If he sees me, he'll keep well away and let someone else do his dirty work for him. Besides, the thunder of the sea will drown out my voice. And there are plenty of rocks about here for him to tie us to. He'd be spoilt for choice. Think it's Christmas come early." Dom shivered at the very thought.

"Let's move on, Muirne," he suggested.

Tell me the Secret

"Where to? Planning saves time. You mentioned dogs and bones. Explain, please." They were near the cliff edge and the rushing wall of water seemed to tower high in the air as a great wave hit the rocks below and seemed to curl back on itself. The tower flume came crashing down upon them. Dom spat out the salty water and thought he would never be dry again.

"Muirne," he said when the roar in his ears had subsided, " that hound belonging to Fionn mac Cumhaill."

"Bran?" said Muirne.

"Bran, that's the one. The other one seems to stick to his master like glue."

"Glue?" Dom just shrugged and hurried on.

"Later. Anyway, Muirne, when we were climbing up with Conall, I noticed that that dog was over there digging. Now what does that suggest to you?"

"Two words, Dom, 'bones' and 'burying'."

"Exactly, Muirne."

"But we're not looking for a dinosaur bone," said Muirne becoming slightly irritated.

"Very funny," said Dom not laughing. "Now, do you want to hear my theory or not?"

"I'm listening," said Muirne softly. Dom was right. She could see he was convinced there was some merit in his idea. "Tell me."

"Dogs just like burying things, any kind of thing." Muirne began to see where he was going with this.

"Like bits of rowan trees?" she suggested.

"Is Fionn's wand of office made of wood from the rowan tree?" he asked.

"The traditional tree planted to ward off evil spirits. It is definitely made of that. Some are made of hazel wood but not this one, I've heard. It's always wrapped in a white woollen cloth and packed along with rowan berries."
Muirne had a feeling she knew where this was heading.
"I think Bran's stolen it, cloth and all, and buried the lot, just where I saw him digging. Just right over there - well, somewhere over there. I was quite a distance away but it was in this general area."
"That could be a problem, Dom, on the mainland or on a more fertile island as it is a bit vague. But not on Staffa. There's not much soil here so any disturbance is likely to have taken place in a very small area. Do you agree, Dom?"
"Absolutely!"
"Like maybe over there for it's the only likely place around," suggested Muirne.
"Bet I get there first," said Dom.
"Some hope," shouted Muirne for she was already on her way, flying like the wind over the sea-soaked surface, dodging in and out of warriors as each one's eyes were riveted on the tiny spaces where each hexagon slotted into its neighbour. Dom could not stop feeling he had entered a nightmarish world of solid shapes that were out to get him as he urged his legs to greater speed over the wet lichen. Muirne had sprinted ahead of him but she had now stopped and was minutely examining every centimetre of coarse, grassy ground in front of her.
"Any luck?" They had only just begun searching but Dom was desperate to know the third element of their quest. Muirne shook her soaking-wet hair.

Tell me the Secret

"I can see where Bran's been digging," she called to Dom. "Looks like it's a hobby of his when he visits Staffa. But there's hardly any soil so he hasn't buried anything deep down."

"Like a wand of office, you mean?" said Dom dispirited. Muirne stopped looking. Dom kept on going.

"Dom, there's very little method to this. Look at all of Fionn's people. Probably at least four of them have searched that same spot. And that is repeated all over the island. A waste of time and effort, that's all this is," said Muirne as she looked about her. Dom stopped looking too.

"So what other way is there?" he asked. "It seems to me that if the dog didn't bury it, then it must have slipped in amongst all the topsy-turvy slabs. Always assuming it was Bran who stole it."

"They should mark each sector off and do it methodically," said Muirne in a very disapproving tone. Dom knew she was probably right.

"It's the time factor. We're not the only ones up against it, you know," lectured Dom. "They have very little time before the role-call of chiefs and chieftains is complete and they're beginning to panic. I for one know how they feel," he said loudly, frowning at Muirne. "Looks like even heroic legends can be human sometimes." His little acidic comment was not lost on Muirne but she said nothing for a few moments.

"Where's Conall?" she eventually asked Dom. "He's with Fionn's people most of the time. He must know Fionn's habits. Let's find him, Dom, and see if we can winkle out a clue."

"Good idea. I last saw him running in that direction, towards the cliff."

"Maybe Fionn had walked there earlier," Muirne suggested, "while he was watching out for the ships to arrive. What do you think, Dom?"

"It's possible. I think it overlooks the entrance to a smaller cave. At least from the spray spouting up, it must be less rugged than the others. Maybe he made his way down."

"But still lethal if you fall," Muirne added. Dom nodded in agreement.

"Come on, Muirne, what have we to lose? 'Tell me the secret.' We've been trying to find the answer to that all the time we've been on Staffa. Now we're just trying to find someone to say it to." It was all beginning to seem pretty hopeless to Dom but he knew Muirne would simply never give up. Or let him for that matter.

Muirne was already carefully making her to the edge. By this time everyone else had moved to the other side of the near-barren island, including Fionn with both his wolf-hounds, Bran and Sgeolan, it seemed.

"If that Bran just chucked the wand over the side, I'll." But Muirne quickly interrupted Dom who would have run a mile if either one of the wolf-hounds had come bounding towards him.

"Now that we'll never know, Dom. But something else has met its fate on the slabs below.

"What?" Dom raced over with dread in his heart.

"Exactly. That's what I said. It's a 'something' not a 'someone', so relax. Well, for a second or two anyway until we work this one out." But Dom did not want to believe his eyes.

Tell me the Secret

"That's Connal's harp," he shouted into the wind which was much stronger nearer the sea.

"Certainly looks like it," agreed Muirne thoughtfully. "It's smashed to pieces." Dom looked helplessly at her.

"How could that have happened, Muirne? And where's Conall. He'd never allow himself to be parted from his harp." He now avoided looking at her as he spoke. The horror of what might have happened to Conall was too dreadful to contemplate and he did not want to see that Muirne might be thinking the same thing too.

"One thing is certain, Dom, and that is there's no way he would have just thrown it down onto the rocks for it to be smashed to bits like this."

"Maybe the wind caught it," Dom suggested hopefully.

"A harp is heavy. It's not a flower that can easily be blown out of a person's hand," said Muirne. "He must have fallen." That bare truth seemed to make life stand still. If Conall had fallen? But neither Dom nor Muirne could bring themselves to voice that idea out loud. Muirne's keen eyes scrutinised every centimetre of the cliff face.

"Do you see him? Anything?" asked Dom, fearful of what the answer might be yet still needing to know. Maybe Conall had been dragged out to sea by the receding waves once their energy was spent on the towering, razor-sharp columns lining the cave and its entrance. Dom and Muirne both tried to blot out that picture from their mind's eye. Muirne shook her head.

"Nothing! Only the smashed harp. Some pieces of its frame are being tossed about by the waves. See? There amongst the foam?" she asked Dom.

"But of Conall?"

Tell me the Secret

"Nothing, Dom, no sign at all. Wait a minute!" Muirne grabbed his arm. "I'm going down. You wait here!" she shouted above the noise of the angry sea.
"You can't, Muirne, you'll be blown off the cliff-side. The wind's too gusty. Muirne, wait and I'll get help."
"We don't need that - yet," she added. "It's just something red. Look straight down and to the right."
"Blood?" He dreaded the answer. All he could see was what looked like a stain the size of an orange. Dom was still holding Muirne back.
"What if it is?" she said, "ignoring it won't make it go away. Looks like it's attached to some clothing. I'm going down. Wait here and if I need help with anything, I'll call out. Now, let go!" Muirne pulled her arm from Dom's hold and waited until a giant blanket of spray had washed over them. She wiped the sea-water from her eyes and carefully lowered herself down along the path cut into the basalt blocks. It was very wet and cold and slippery but she kept her eyes firmly on the red bundle some way down. She could make out the beautiful eternal knot carving on the topmost part of the harp's smashed frame as it was carried in and out by the foaming brine below.
"Are you alright?" Dom shouted anxiously from above.
"Fine!" Muirne replied but stopped to hold on tightly to a niche in the columns as the waves raced in erratically yet again. She was close now, almost close enough to touch the cloth. She heard noises above and knew without looking up that Fionn mac Cumhaill was there watching anxiously with Dom.

    Muirne huddled over the campfire to get some of its warmth. Her fingers had been so cold she could still not believe she had managed to hold onto the wand as she had climbed back up again.

"Berries! Rowan berries! Not blood!" said Dom for what seemed to Muirne to be the one hundredth time. Dom watched as she slipped the berries into the pouch beside the others. Some souvenir, he thought. "Not a dead or injured body in sight," he said sounding quite disappointed and eating another spoonful of horrible stew.

"I was truly sorry to disappoint you, Dom," teased Muirne.

"Me? I was definitely not disappointed," he protested strongly. Berries, not blood. He could still hear Fionn laughing at that one. "A bit much, though, that the great warrior forgot his promise immediately, I think. Just grabbed the wand and strode off without saying a word of thanks never mind the promise of the secrets of the universe being revealed."

"That's celebrities for you," said Muirne. "But he did say something, be fair, Dom." Dom looked puzzled. "He told you to take the wolf-hounds for a walk until they had done their business." Muirne tried hard not to laugh at Dom's expression.

"That man's never heard of poop-scoops."

"There, there, now, you must remember that Fionn mac Cumhaill's a free spirit. He flits between worlds when and as it takes his fancy and dogs dirt quite possibly doesn't exist for him. Probably moves on to the next world to avoid being asked to pick it up," Muirne suggested with a straight face.

"Well, I took Bran and Sgeolan for their walk and I can tell you it exists for them." Dom screwed up his face at the very recent memory.

Tell me the Secret

"Did you tell Bran you were sorry you blamed him for hiding the wand?" Dom sniffed before answering.

"I didn't think that was necessary for he wasn't present when I mentioned it to you."

"Quite so, Dom. Now, where on earth is Conall? Here one minute to see if you're alright and then he vanishes again."

"Probably gone off with Fionn and the warriors. They're all talking heroic talk and he'll be playing and singing some heroic songs. I'll tell you something, though, that Number 1 harpist is a litter-lout. It's folk like him who pollute the beaches."

"Dom, you've lost me. Who do what?"

"Mess up the beaches. He should have waited until he was back home before he dumped it."

"Oh, the smashed harp, Dom? He didn't dump it. Conall said that Bran got a bit frisky and knocked it out of Number 1 harpist's hands. Seems he was singing to the waves, trying to calm them, when Bran, a free spirit like his master, came bounding up and bowled the poor man over. The harpist had been entrusted with the wand parcel and it went over along with the harp. Seems he was just too scared to own up, Dom."

"Muirne, Staffa has been a dead loss. I must have got it wrong. Let's have a look at your father's plan and see what's next."

"What's next is a song, my friends." Conall sat down beside them and smiled.

"Can't you see we're busy," said Dom sharply. "Away you go and see if you've more luck that your boss at calming the waves. 'Tell me the secret.' Don't suppose you could do

Tell me the Secret

that before you go?" Conall cleared his throat quietly and prepared to sing.

"Right, it goes like this. 'I am the pale moon.'" He really did have a beautiful voice, thought Muirne. "That do? The Mariota one? Was that it? Now, any requests? I'm right up on heroic ones these days, naturally." Dom and Muirne were now speechless. "Can see I'm wasting my time here. I'm off, folks." In a daze, they watched Conall go. Dom was first to recover.

"So much for having to overcome evil to get the answer! Got it wrong there big-time. So, Muirne, what do we have here? The riddle and the answers to it?"

"More or less, I think. 'I begin at the end .' 'I am nothing.' 'I am the pale moon' from Conall. Oh, how I wish that sea would stop churning so that I can think this through," said Muirne. "If only we could figure out what it all means. Dom, what have we to show for all the terrible things that have happened to us?"

"Personally, Muirne, I thought the salmon sail was terrific." Muirne pretended not to hear.

"We have three mysterious lines, a button, a pebble and some berries. One berry, I should say, for I mixed the rest into Anluann's brew by mistake. It's alright, Dom, it won't do him any harm." That pacified Dom somewhat for he had become quite fond of the little fellow.

"We still have the plan. Let's see it. This place will be like hundreds of sardines trying to fight their way into a single tin when all those other chiefs arrive with their followers." Muirne carefully removed the plan from its wrapping and they scrutinised it again. Dom turned it round every possible way then shook his head.

Tell me the Secret

"This other long rectangle means nothing, Muirne, sorry." He felt he had let her down. Muirne suddenly laughed.
"We've just solved it, Dom, we really have," she cried.
"Eh?"
"Look. The three lines of the riddle. 'I begin at the end.' means a circle. 'I am nothing.' means just that - nothing, another circle. 'I am the pale moon.' is yet another one. Three circles and these three," said Muirne holding out the palm of her hand for him to see. "The button, the pebble and the berry are all circles too."
"Which means?" asked Dom still more confused than ever.
"Your interpretation of Father's plan has been correct all along. It has led us to where we are in the quest today. This long, rectangle we're on is Staffa and its magnificent columns. The other one beside it indicates columns too, only much smaller ones." She looked at Dom and laughed as his face showed the dawning of understanding.
"The standing stones!" he yelled. "Ardalanish!"
"Absolutely right. And there we'll find a very special little stone with even smaller holes in it and we will be able to fit these three into them. Then we shall all be free and Mariota will have her very own little stone back. For that's what this is all about, Dom, returning a fairy stone to its original owner so that she can be free too."
"How do you know that there is a stone, Muirne? That it has three holes in it? That it's all to do with Mariota?"
"Very simple. Mother once told me she put it there within the sacred circle."
"But it's not that simple, is it?" The chilling laughter that accompanied these words filled Dom's and Muirne's hearts

Tell me the Secret

with dread. "You will have to defeat us first." Dom and Muirne were rooted to the spot.

"Gorach!" boomed out Fionn mac Cumhaill's voice and the air seemed to shake. "A word. Now!"

"Dom, run! Run!" They did, But where to? There was no escape.

chapter 14

Muirne looked down as the sea boiled beneath them. Where to run? Where to hide?

"At least on Staffa we're safe from the Golkani," said Dom trying to keep from slipping off the slippery surface and into the writhing sea below.

"Fionn will not have any of them about with their constant bickering. It'll be difficult enough for him to keep the peace among all those rival warriors without that."

"So, Muirne, do you think Gorach has positioned them where he can summon them the moment he leaves Staffa?"

Muirne nodded.

"That would be my guess, Dom."

"We're in a right fix," he said.

"We're stuck on this island and there's no way off. Even if we had a boat, it would be the same scenario as this morning on the other one. Let's face it, we don't actually figure in Fionn's plans at all," said Muirne.

"In spite of the fact that you found his wand of office?" Dom said bitterly.

"Seems like heroes have short memories. Fionn's only concerned with what happens right now here on Staffa. We're small fry to him, Dom. We're on our own once again."

"So we're well and truly stuck and Gorach knows it." Muirne just shrugged as she spoke.

"He's probably off wolfing down one of those burger-look-alikes while Fionn talks to him," said Dom. "Actually, Muirne, I think mine was turnip and barley seeds." Dom shuddered at the very thought. "Is it a bit cold here or is it just me?"

"The sun's beginning to set. That and the icy sea-water drenching us on this ledge might just be the cause. What do you think?" Dom was not very sure.

"I think I'm hallucinating, Muirne. Starvation does that to you. I'm told it makes you imagine things."

"Like what?" Muirne shivered, too. Dom was right about the chill in the air.

"Like the sea below us gradually easing back to the point of vanishing."

"Sounds bad. Is there a cure?" she asked.

"Don't know but would you care to look down?" Muirne pulled a face and then decided maybe she should humour him. He should never have had that beaker of mead. It was probably still making him woozy. "Just a quick look, Muirne. Costs nothing." Muirne looked down and then looked back up sharply at Dom.

"I don't believe this!"

"Well, I do and I'm going to jump down there and run like a hare. I'm not looking for explanations, heroic tales, Celtic gods and goddesses. That's more in your line of thinking.

Just let me reach one of those wagons before - if this really is a dream - before I wake up. Coming?"

The Sound of Iona with its turbulent currents and waves boiling and crashing around Staffa's breathtaking basalt columns had been transformed into a vast, fertile plain. A long line of wagons and carts, horsemen cantering and children frolicking, slowly made their way down the grassy, flower-filled meadow that had once been the azure-blue sea. Its emerald tints were now green-leaved trees, its foam-tipped waves now swaying, ripening corn. The waves had piled up behind this wonderful sight and only became rushing waters again once it had passed. The sea seemed to be a part of the procession, dancing along behind it. Riding at the head in his golden chariot stood a proud, magnificent, green-clad figure, a golden crown on his head. He was as tall almost as Fionn and he smiled as he and his people made their way slowly along. Muirne ran as fast as she could and caught up with Dom as he hauled himself into the nearest wagon. Behind them, the waters of the Sound of Iona boiled and bubbled like a joyful, living wall and followed the incredible procession south.

"Where to? Where are you going?" Dom asked the driver as he hauled Muirne on board.

"We're off to Islay. I like going there. Very hospitable people there. Make great tablet." Dom stomach rumbled loudly as the smiling driver spoke.

"So you'll be passing near Loch na Lathaich?" he asked hopefully.

"Of course. Have some oat bars, friends." Dom thought his luck was definitely improving. Even Muirne took one.

Tell me the Secret

"Who is your leader, that great warrior in his magnificent chariot?" she asked. She accepted a handful of hazel nuts as she gazed at the incredible spectacle about her. The man laughed.

"You don't recognise him?" The man had great difficulty in believing that and shook his head in disbelief.

"He's Manannan mac Lir, the son of the sea god Lir. Some say, though, Manannan does not like to get wet so he parts the sea rather than sail on it. Suits me." Muirne smiled for everyone had heard of the great Manannan mac Lir and Gorach would definitely not try to touch them while they were with his party. Dom nudged Muirne and pointed south towards the horizon, towards the hills of Jura. A black mass hovered there menacingly. So that was where Gorach had told the Golkani to stay while he went to Staffa.

"Hope Fionn keeps Gorach at the talks till we reach the standing stones at Ardalanish, Muirne," he whispered.

"Fionn just seemed to want a word with Gorach, Dom. He's got no reason to keep him any longer, it would seem. For the present anyway. Gorach probably thinks he can take care of his little problem - us - and be back on Staffa by the time the talks with the other leaders get underway." Dom looked glum.

"Nothing's changed then? We'll not be safe until we place the three objects into the three little holes in the stone which we don't actually have yet?" Muirne nodded in agreement.

"And that means back to where we started at the standing stones."

"Not quite back to where we started, Muirne. You're forgetting the small matter of a boat-wreck. I think that came first." Muirne smiled sweetly at him.

"Just put it down to experience," she advised.

"That's right. Just a very sharp, really painful and extremely steep learning curve," said Dom, his eyes still on the Golkani.

"Now, Dom, this is all very pleasant but we really must make our way to Ardalanish. Those little boys and girls we fondly call the Golkani seem to be moving slightly closer by the minute."

"No problem." Dom turned back to the wagon-driver. "I heard those men on horseback say they were going to leave Manannan's procession and head inland. Is that right?" The man nodded and bit into an oat bar. Dom forced himself to concentrate on staying alive long enough to enjoy a decent meal. "Any chance they would take us and drop us off at Loch na Lathaich?" Dom could see that right then, it was a stretch of water that no longer existed as the loch had been temporarily swallowed up by Manannan mac Lir's plain.

"Don't see why not for that's their usual route. Have you ridden a horse before? Or are you just willing to hang on like grim death for a short time?"

"The latter," said Muirne. "My friend's into sharp, learning curves."

"I've a horrible feeling that it's going to be a very painful, sharp learning curve," said Dom.

"Doesn't bother me," said Muirne, "but if it bothers you, well." The challenge was there and Dom could do nothing but take it up.

"Not at all," he said loudly and hoped he sounded like he meant it.

"If they drop us off at my village, which will not be there, of course."

"You never know, Muirne, for it's a good place to trade," said Dom interrupting.

"Maybe, but we won't count on getting any help there. If they drop us off there then we can easily make our way the short distance over to the standing stones. I think that's the best plan at the moment. Agreed, Dom?" she said.

"Agreed. Think Mariota will be there? he asked.

"I hope so but we must make sure Anluann's not too sleepy so he'll be ready to help. No more lavender for him," Muirne decided.

"Still got the button, pebble and berry?"

"Is this you ticking off a check-list, Dom? Have you still got your fluff-covered oat bar? Anluann?" Dom nodded.

"I'll go and ask these guys for a lift. They look like they're about to set off," said Dom jumping down and making his way to a group of fierce-looking horse-men. Muirne watched as he talked and pointed to the dark, high bens of Mull and Muirne began to get anxious. The Golkani cloud had vanished. She felt that it would be no time at all before they would see them circling and swooping, screaming and screeching. They were safe for the moment with Manannan mac Lir but they could not remain there forever. Suddenly Dom waved to her. Muirne ran quickly over and climbed up behind one of the riders. They were racing across the plain within minutes and Muirne and Dom were both glad that Manannan, son of Lir, the god of the sea, did not like water.

They watched and waved farewell until the thunder and dust of the hoof-beats faded to nothing. Cattle roamed the fields beside them and the faint sound of sobbing began to fill the air. A young girl came running up to them, begging for help. Dom was filled with a sudden dread.

"Be very careful, Murine," he cautioned. "Don't trust her."

"She's just a girl and it looks like she needs our help," said Muirne, "we can't just pass by." But Dom had a feeling, a horrible feeling, that Gorach was right there with them.

chapter 15

"I don't like this!"

"Rubbish, Dom, when did you get the second sight?" asked Muirne scathingly.

"We're just about there, Muirne, the end of the quest. Why waste time now?"

"Waste time? Was that what you were thinking when you offered to help me? Better than watching the waves breaking on the shore on Iona? Well, thanks for nothing, mate." Muirne's temper was a little frayed. Dom gave in.

"All right, keep your hair on. It's just a feeling. I'm probably a bit wound up, not thinking straight, suspicious of everything and."

"Yes, Dom, I get the message. You've had enough. Well, so have I and probably Anluann feels the same way too. But let's just hang in there for a little while longer. No arguments. We're a team, remember?" Dom smiled reluctantly and sighed loudly.

"I suppose allotting five minutes of our precious time to helping the girl won't make much difference," he said and hoped like mad the girl was just fed up and did not actually need more than a few kind words. But was that a little, muted screech he heard? He looked about him but the air was fresh and clear. He hoped Muirne had not seen him give a start. She would think him a real wimp.

The girl had now sat down on a raised patch of short grass at the edge of an flat piece of land overlooking the loch. Manannan mac Lir had passed and all was back to normal. Dom had been disappointed that there had been not huts, no village by the side of the water. They could see the standing stones' outlines etched solidly against the horizon. Muirne silently admitted to herself that she too wished the girl had not been there and that they could have hurried straight on. She looked keenly around her. The sky was clear, the deep orange and pinks of sunset beginning to streak the late afternoon sky above the horizon. She knew there really was not much time left for them to complete their quest. It was all so easily within their reach. This had to be hurried along. The cattle within the field chewed contentedly on the lush grass, wandering slowly as they went along. But why was the girl crying? She was wiping her eyes with the hem of the coarse, linen apron that she had put on over her long, brown, woollen dress. Her two brown plaits framed her small, oval-shaped face and were tied at the ends with strips of a deep, green cloth. Muirne hurried up to speak to her. Dom stayed a little way off. Crying girls were not his idea of good causes. Old women needing help to carry a heavy bags, yes. Mums with babies and heavy bags, yes again. But girls his own age just crying?

No. Experience had taught him that in these situations, he just made matters worse. He continued to stay back.

"What's wrong?" Muirne asked, sitting close by the girl. The girl did her best to stop crying as she spoke.

"I've lost our piglet."

"How did you manage that?" called Dom with his usual lack of tact. Muirne glared at him.

"Tell us how it happened. Did something scare it and it ran off?" she asked sympathetically.

"Yes, I think it must have got a fright. I was in the cottage and there was this sudden bang. Don't know yet what caused it. The hens and pigs scattered all over the place and when I got them back and counted them, the littlest piglet was missing. I've searched everywhere," said the girl and, once more, dissolved into tears.

"Oh don't worry. It has to be somewhere. We'll help you look for it," said Muirne, "won't we Dom?"

"Definitely," he agreed with the best smile he could muster, for the look on Muirne's face was an order not a request. Would not take long anyway, he thought, for the ground was flat and dipped a bit here and there but there was nothing that could be called a knoll never mind a hill. Dom had remembered that he was part of a team. "If it's here, we'll find it."

"Thank you." That had cheered the girl up a little.

"Pigs squeal, don't they?" said Dom. "That should make it quite easy to track the piglet down."

"Where have you looked already?" asked Muirne.

"Mainly just by that dip over there. There are plenty of gorse bushes it can hide in but it's not there." Dom wondered if a little piglet was capable of playing hide and seek.

"Won't it just be wanting something to eat? Maybe its little snout has led it back home again," he suggested. Dom and Muirne were now anxiously looking for the piglet but the girl just sat where she was.

"Would help if she got up and did a bit of searching herself," moaned Dom. Muirne brushed his comment aside.

"She's very upset. Just leave her," she said brusquely. But Dom was only half listening to her.

"And her family. Where are they? What are they doing right now?" he said looking about him.

"They don't need to be here. The cattle are taken to the fields and left to fend for themselves." Again Dom was only half-listening to Muirne.

"And have you seen a cottage about here? Just exactly how far can a piglet wander? This little piglet seems to have gone for a hike." Muirne looked at Dom and nodded.

"I'll have a word with her. See if she can be a bit more exact." She called the girl over. Time was flying past. Maybe, thought Muirne, they could come back again and help. "Let's have a chat with her, Dom. Maybe we could just call in at the cottage and explain what happened. Make sure they're not angry with her. Explain that it wasn't her fault."

"Great idea," he said with relief. "Muirne, you know that Fionn's rivals must surely be on Staffa by this time and Gorach won't stay there forever. Aw, wait a minute. Over there!" Dom laughed suddenly. "So much for my intuition." The piglet roamed free in amongst the legs of the cattle. "I'll get it. You wait there in case it bolts again." It was

Tell me the Secret

pale pink, fat and as cute as a bag of monkeys leading Dom a merry dance as it ran deeper into the herd.

"It knows you're chasing it," shouted Muirne enjoying the spectacle before her. "Just be careful you don't get trampled by the cows. And watch out the piglet doesn't get hurt either," she warned. Dom suddenly felt guilty and backed away a little. The piglet seemed to hesitate but then followed him.

"I'll grab him when we're both clear," he called over to Muirne. "Look, isn't he lovely?"

"Now I don't think that's the right word for me." The voice came from close by and Dom's feet refused to move as his brain ceased to send them any messages.

"Gorach!" Dom heard Muirne's warning cry and, somewhere in the depths of his mind, he wondered why the piglet was called Gorach. The awful form seemed to rear up before him as the piglet transformed itself into Dom's worst nightmare.

"Run, Muirne," Dom managed to shout as his senses returned, "they are here! The Gokani!" The fiends appeared, laughing and swooping, enjoying their freedom now that they were no longer hindered by the shape of cattle.

Dom ran faster than he had ever done before in his life and hoped the few minutes gained while the Golkani and Gorach were enjoying the joke would be enough to find shelter. Muirne had vanished. Also the girl. Where were they? He looked about him frantically.

"Here! Over here and get right down!" Dom dived under an old water trough. "Easy! Don't scatter the sheep!" said Muirne. Dom crouched down beside her and they mingled with the flock of sheep that crowded around the trough in the sheep-fank. "The Golkani will be everywhere trying to track us down once they've had their laugh."

"Where's the girl?" asked Dom and Muirne managed a rueful grin. In her eyes, it served as an apology.

"You were right, Dom." He just nodded.

"Did I really catch the tiniest glimpse of a crystal boat on the loch as I ran here?" he asked but he already knew the answer.

"I think she and Gorach are a team as well." They both smiled in spite of the situation they were now in. "We're in a real mess this time, I'm afraid, Dom." He just brushed that comment aside.

"We've been in a real mess from the start," he said. "We've managed so far."

"We've wriggled out quite successful," Muirne agreed with some pride in her voice.

"And straight into another one," added Dom with an honesty they could easily have done without. "Somehow, Muirne, I don't think you father's plan will get us out of this one."

"But maybe Anluann will."

"How?" asked Dom hopefully and warily at the same time.

"I don't know yet. But we've only got one last chance to use him for, if we can't get him back, we will have nothing left to threaten Gorach with in order to reach the standing stones."

"So what do you suggest, Muirne? Use him or lose him." Dom waited in silence although his ears were listening out for the dreaded noise of the Golkani. He knew Muirne was weighing up every angle.

Tell me the Secret

"Are you any good at herding sheep?" she whispered suddenly. Dom was startled.

"I'd probably make a good sheep-dog but a rotten shepherd. I know how the dogs work. My own dog Wodin is a collie-dog," said Dom proudly. What he did not say that Wodin had failed his sheep rounding-up exam and that was why he was now Dom's pet. A collie-dog school drop-out. But Dom reckoned that as far as information was concerned right then, less was definitely more. There was no need to depress Muirne.

"Then I think I might just have an idea," she said quietly as the sheep milled about them.

"I'm listening," said Dom and that he was and very intently too. Whether he had a future or not depended completely on this. The screeching was now coming very close and would be on them in seconds. The sound did not disturb the sheep much for they just moved around a little more closely together. Dom and Muirne crouched even further beneath the large wooden trough and well out of sight. Muirne whispered urgently to Dom.

"The Golkani are not going to leave the area. They know we are here somewhere and they can also see the standing stones quite clearly. They'll settle for patrolling the area until time will force us into flight. There's not much cover between here and the sacred circle so they'll have plenty of time to pick us off."

"Thanks for that bit of news. Is it the good news and then the bad or the bad news and then the even worse?" said Dom.

"Well, it's good news in a way for the lie of the land will make them over-confident."

"With good reason," commented Dom.
"It's not that bad, Dom. Listen, all we have to do is herd these lovely woolly friends of our to within a very short distance of the sacred circle and then just a step or two and we'll have made it."
"Great - if it works. You know, Muirne, I think it just might. You realise we'll be stinking to high-heaven at the end of it." Muirne smiled her sweetest smile.
"Stinking but safe, Dom, safe."

chapter 16

Muirne edged her way to the head of the flock nearest the direction they wanted to travel take. Dom eased his way along, gently prodding on both sides as he went. Fortunately the sheep were none to clean and Dom's and Muirne's clothes melted into the flock.
"Collect as much wool as you can as we go along," she had whispered just as they had separated and Dom, puzzled, decided that Muirne had an idea that might at some point require sheep's coats. The smell was horrendous and he was glad he had not eaten much that day for his stomach was doing its best to heave out its contents. He knew that the dyke surrounding the fank was slowly approaching - along with the sunset - but Dom tried not to think of that. Unless he timed it right, he would stand out like a sore thumb when the sheep leapt over it. The Golkani would then have their quarry. He was surprised at how little

attention the sheep paid to the screaming and diving but he had no time to give it much thought. The wall came up and keeping as low as possible and performing a neat forward roll in amongst a group of bleating sheep, Dom found himself outside and onto the narrow track that led to the standing stones. He fervently hoped the owner of the sheep was too busy elsewhere to notice his livelihood was on the move. Being herded back into the sheep-fank did not appeal to him one bit.

"Oh no!" The sound was out before he could stop it.

"Shh! Shh!" He could tell Muirne was furious with him.

"I've just knelt in."

"Too much information, Dom," she whispered back at him, " now shut up and crawl. Don't forget the wool." Dom took the rather forceful hint.

"All right, Bossy Boots," he mouthed at her back as she crawled straight ahead, leading the sheep forward and staying well-hidden amongst them. Easy for her, he thought, for she was small and slightly built. He was big for his age and liked his food. An idea suddenly struck him and he grabbed the two biggest and fattest sheep on either side of him and they moved on as a threesome, side by side. The first few grabs at their coats had only resulted in handfuls of wool, so he stuffed them into his pockets. That would put him back into Muirne's good books. Dom was careful not to waken Anluann.

"Leave no stone unturned, Golkani people." Dom stumbled at the booming sound of Gorach's voice. But his sheep-mates just kept on going, trailing him through little mounds of steaming droppings and warm wet stuff. The whirring and screeching was now everywhere as the Golkani obeyed their leader and renewed their search with vigour. Dom buried himself deep into the sheep's coats and hoped for the best. There were no triumphant whoops of joy and the sheep kept moving along the track so Dom knew Muirne had not been discovered. He fervently wished he could see what was happening. He wanted so badly to talk to Muirne. They could cheer each other up. Suddenly, all was quiet. Dom waited. The sheep looked about them. He wondered what they saw. He could only wait for Muirne to say if they were anywhere near the circle. Murne's face appeared before him.

"Go back, Muirne, the sheep will scatter," he said in as low a voice as possible. Why on earth had she deserted her post. He was filled with dread. She shook her head.

"No they won't. There's a small dyke ahead and some grass on this side of it that will keep the leaders in their place. We only have about fifty metres to go till we reach the sacred circle but it's all open ground."

"Meaning we'll be sitting targets the moment we're in the open," said Dom nervously.

"Exactly," agreed Muirne.

"Yes, but we won't be in the open for long for the sheep will cover us till we get there and then we can shoo them away." Muirne shook her head.

"We must respect the sacred circle and we can't take the chance the sheep will be willing to forsake the lush grass they'll see there. We've no time to hang about trying to persuade them to go back home. The standing stones themselves would be at risk for sheep like to scratch their bodies against anything hard. We can't allow that, Dom, we can't be the cause of them being scratched. We'll have

Tell me the Secret

to leave them here behind the wall." Muirne peered through the woolly coats. "The sky's clear and the sun is setting fast. Now here's what we'll do," she whispered.

"Hope it's a good idea," said Dom in hushed tones.

"Good, bad or indifferent, Dom, it's all we've got. Now, untie your laces and you'd best throw the pouches away for they'll only make you trip."

"Why should that happen? They've worked perfectly well so far," he protested.

"Because there will be nothing attaching them to your feet. Untie your laces." Dom did as he was told - reluctantly. "Now make the wool into a firm ball. That's right, all of it but not too tight as we want a bit of air going through it. That and the oil from the sheep will help. Good. Use your lace, like this," said Muirne as she was doing exactly the same with the wool she had collected, "and attach it to the ball. Leave about this length free so that we can swing them round our heads in a huge circle." Dom shook his head.

"And Gorach's going to be scared to death by a ball of wool," he whispered. "Muirne, I hope you don't mind my saying this, for I know you're doing your best, but this ranks Number 1 in the list of completely no-hoper ideas chart." Muirne simply ignored his comment.

"And if, well, probably when, the Golkani attack," she continued, " we'll use Anluann to light the wool and wave it about to scare them off. They hate heat and smoke as you know. That was a great idea of yours on Ulva. Did I say that?"

"No you did not!"

"Anyway, while we're whirling the smoke and fire bombs about, we keep moving towards the circle. It's a short distance but a crucial one. What do you think?" she asked still whispering and watching the lead sheep.

"I think your idea has just slipped down the list of duff ones. It might even work. In fact, Muirne, I think that together, as a team, we can make it work. We'll go for it."

"Always pays never to interrupt, Dom," said Muirne feeling very pleased.

"My apologies. I was too hasty, Muirne. Now what?" he asked. Suddenly, Muirne and Dom were alone, sheep racing away in all directions as a monstrous pillar of fire leapt up before them. Gorach! They had forgotten that although he was their leader, he was not a Golkani, he had no fear of fire. The Golkani were nearby but not right beside them.

"Light the wool, Dom! Quick! Before the fire dies. Try not to lose hold of Anluann for we don't have time to recover him. We have to get past Gorach before the fire dies. He won't like the smoke." Muirne shouted the instructions as she ran towards the dying fountain of fire. Dom was close on her heels, tying off the lace as he went. One run past did it. Anluann wriggled in his hand as the balls were now smoking and shooting sparks everywhere and, moments later, Gorach, as himself, stood not in front, but behind them. The ground between them and the sacred circle was clear. They turned to face him. But he was laughing and fear coursed through Dom and Muirne as they backed away, still swinging the balls round their heads.

"What does he know that we don't, Muirne?" asked Dom nervously.

"Just that although he's in front of us as we're backing off, the Golkani are now massed behind us. We now have another barrier between us and the standing stones." They swung their fire-balls fiercely at Gorach as he tried to approach.

"But surely they'll scatter as the fire-balls come nearer?" Muirne glanced quickly behind her at the silent, still Golkani.

"I hope so, " she said, " so just keep on moving and watching both behind and in front. Let's go." They moved again, eyes everywhere, constantly roving as the Golkani now began their screaming and swooping, their razor-sharp, lethal weapons dangling from their finger-tips ready to slice anything they touched. A determined lunge from Muirne and Dom kept them at bay but both of them knew it could not last. The fire would eventually burn out and they would be left defenceless. Muirne began to feel her arms losing their strength as the Golkani relentlessly tried to pierce their defences.

"Keep it going as long as possible," she urged.

"Will do. This lot will have to give way to the fire when we reach the edge of the sacred circle." Dom kept on hurling the fireball about him as he shouted to Muirne. They each knew what the other was thinking. The Golkani were no fools, just crazy beings with an even crazier leader in Gorach. But they knew that the more they harried, the slower would be the progress Dom and Muirne would make. They also knew the fireballs could not last for any great length of time and then Dom and Muirne would be totally at their mercy.

Tell me the Secret

"Anluann is our only hope, Muirne," shouted Dom above the terrible noise, the shrill screeching pounding endlessly in their brains. The oiled wool was producing smoke but the Golkani were everywhere. Suddenly, the fireballs spluttered and died.

"Gorach!" shouted Muirne, "we'll fire Anluann directly at you if you don't call off the Golkani and let us enter the sacred circle of stones." Gorach hesitated.

"No you won't!" No-one moved, not Muirne, not Dom, not Gorach nor one single Golkani as Anluann spoke. Suddenly there was uproar as the Golkani cheered Anluann's decision not to help their enemies.

"Quiet!" shouted Gorach, moving slowly forward towards Muirne and Dom who held Anluann fast in his hand. "Welcome home, little friend, welcome Anluann. Come here, back to your family."

"No!" said Anluann.

"What?" shouted Gorach, his smarmy voice changing to one of fury. "What did you say?"

"I've decided to retire. Well, that's not quite accurate for I've one last, very pleasant duty to perform then maybe a relaxing cruise around the best-known and very active volcanoes." Anluann smiled at the thought of it.

"Are you mad? Have you forgotten who you're talking to?" said Gorach threateningly.

"I have not, Gorach."

"Oh I think you have." Gorach stepped very close to Dom and Dom felt his hand shake a little but he still kept a firm grip of Anluann.

"Sorry to disagree but I actually haven't," said Anluann. "And will you please loosen your grip." Dom did as he was asked. "You see, everybody, my whole life consists of work then sleep then work again and on it goes and I've had enough. I'm opting out of the rat-race."

"Well you'd better think of opting in again before I do something drastic," Gorach threatened.

"I don't think so, Gorach. The tour's all booked. Paid for last week. I'm off. You guys are on your own. But, as I said, just one very pleasant duty to perform and then it's goodbye to all this aggro. I am now Mr Nice Guy. It's a long-standing tradition, as well you know, Gorach, that I light and lead in the firebrand at Fionn mac Cumhaill's Staffa bun-fight. I do believe you've received your invitation, too, Gorach, and this time Fionn, with his legendary bad taste, has also invited the Golkani on condition they haven't annihilated anyone within the last two days and will behave themselves while eating. Spitting is definitely out!" He smiled broadly at Muirne and Dom.

"I think we'll just have a seat by the tall standing stone," said Dom, "while you and your Golkani go partying, Gorach." Anluann vanished out of his hand.

"Me? Leave you two and go to a party?" roared Gorach.

"That's what our master expects. He sent us to make sure you come, Gorach." Bran and Sgeolan sniffed menacingly round Gorach's legs. Gorach and his Golkani discovered quite suddenly that they were indeed party animals.

chapter 17

Dom and Muirne watched the black mass rise, circle reluctantly above and then leave, still squabbling.

"I expect Fionn mac Cumhaill will sort the Golkani and Gorach out, don't you, Muirne?" said Dom. Muirne laughed.

"I expect Conall's singing will be wasted on them," she said. They were both now looking at the standing stones, both wondering where to begin the final search.

"I think we might just beat sunset with an hour or so to spare. You said your mother hid it round here somewhere."

"That's right. Once we find it, I'll insert the button, pebble and berry into the holes and see what happens." Dom suddenly felt a bit anxious.

"Hope they fit," he said. Muirne had the same misgivings but wisely said nothing. "Where do you think we should begin?"

"Anywhere," said Muirne.

"That certainly narrows it down! No clues at all? An hour can pass very quickly when you're just scrambling about aimlessly, Muirne. Think hard." They were both now very tired and thinking was certainly becoming more difficult to do.

"What I know is this. When I was born, Mother met an old lady on the road and she gave the stone as a gift. A Mariota stone, she said. I don't know if Mother guessed it had once belonged to someone called Mariota. The old woman said it was special, had magic powers, would keep me safe."

"And your mother wasn't about to say, 'No thanks'."

"Right. The custom is to bury a gift of that kind somewhere sacred. Could be slipped down a holy well, thrown into a sacred stream, something like that, but in this case, Mother loved the standing stones, and so she buried it here - somewhere. It's the old beliefs that have never quite died out. Celtic people are very superstitious."

"And that was how many years ago?"

"Ten exactly, today" said Muirne.

"So what's happened to trigger this off after all this time?" asked Dom.

"I've no idea."

"Well, something must have done it. Not that it matters now we've almost unravelled the riddle, but it would be interesting to know just the same. You said your father has been working on the stone for about a month or so and that your mother was last seen beside it. Am I right?"

"You are, Dom, but keep on looking while you talk. The stone is more important right now than the reason why this all happened."

"Point taken." They continued to search frantically.

"It's find the stone first and then we can sit back and think about the reason for it all, said Murne frowning. "You look around this one and I'll take the smaller one over there. Mother would definitely have placed it within the sacred circle. No point otherwise."

"Maybe your mother dug it up again, Muirne. Maybe that's what's angered those folk in the other world."

"If she had done that, it would have been for something extraordinary. But that morning, she was just her usual happy self. No different from any other day."

"Well, somebody did something to start this all off. Any luck where you are?"

"None," said Muirne despondently. Dom looked over at her and wished he could just wave one of those magic wands that seemed to be so commonplace in the world of gods and goddesses.

"What's that discolouration in the ground there. Something must have lain there for a very long time. A rectangle of sorts. Looks like it's been removed not long ago," said Dom wandering over.

"Oh that! That's where the monks of the abbey decided to dig up a stone slab and use it. That's the one Father's working on at St Ernan's. The one he's put the name Mariota on. He wasn't the least bit pleased about having to put whatever the abbot had asked him to inscribe on it. I heard him whispering to Mother. She was giving him some looks that would have frightened the dead. But it was a commission from the abbot and that's who gives him most of his work. We all have to eat. There's nothing there, though, Dom. It was dug up in case it was covering a grave but it wasn't. Nobody had realised it was as long and beautiful as it is. It looked quite plain and was almost completely hidden by grass and earth. The main decoration was on the other side. Probably just abandoned before it was completed so long ago that nobody remembers anything about it."

"Except perhaps your mother because she's from a long line of women who pass that sort of information down through

Tell me the Secret

the generations, isn't she?" said Dom quietly, "and don't worry, I'm still looking."

"What do you mean? Mother told me nothing really," Muirne said sharply. All this talk was getting them nowhere.

"Stop searching just for a moment, Muirne, and listen. Got an idea. Here is this tall stone, there is the smaller one, then you have the spot where the other stone - we'll call it Mariota's stone - was found."

"I can see that. So?"

"So they're in a straight line. Now what's next in that line? Look carefully," said Dom.

"That rocky outcrop! Dom!"

"Muirne, I think your mother knew a lot more than she let on. I think she really did know that stone had been a favourite of the legendary Mariota's- our Mariota - all her life. You said your family have the second sight, the women were each a drui-ban in the past. I think maybe she persuaded your father to inscribe a different name on it from the one the abbot wanted."

"You might just be right, Dom," said Muirne slowly and thoughtfully and waited anxiously for Dom to continue.

"Old stories passed down through the ages, some understood, some their meaning only guessed at. Your mother could have heard all of that round the fire on the dark, Mull nights. What if your father was told all this by your mother and decided that if he carved Mariota's name into the stone, the abbot wouldn't be able to use it and maybe he would just discard it."

"And that way, Father could make sure it was Mariota's for all eternity?" Dom nodded.

Tell me the Secret

"I don't know how Mariota came to be separated from it and the little one but we'll ask her when she appears. I think also that your mother continued the line of the sacred stones and placed your stone right beneath that rock. See, it actually tapers at the bottom. It's very overgrown and the gorse covers it well. It would be an ideal spot where it could lie safe forever or until Mariota came back to claim it." Muirne's eyes widened. She stepped slowly towards it, then turned and looked at Dom.

"Let's do it together."

They both dug furiously with their hands and jumped for joy when the small, sea-smoothed stone gradually appeared. Muirne gently lifted it and they walked silently into the shadow of the taller stone and sat down.

"Three small holes, it's got three small holes!" whispered Dom who was still not convinced they had shaken off the Golkani forever. "Got a definite feeling, Muirne, that we've got the right stone." She nodded, smiling at him.

"So this is the end of our quest, Dom."

"If they all fit," he said as he sat on the grass beside her.

"Only one way to find out," said a quiet voice behind them. Mariota! She sat down beside them, her green tunic blending with the grass, the golden belt glinting in the mellow rays of the dying sun. Her long flaxen hair spilled over her shoulders. "Now, tell me, what are the objects you have found and the answers you've been given to 'Tell me the secret.'" Muirne placed the little stone in her lap and searched her pouch for the three objects. She held them in the upturned palm of her small hand as Dom repeated the answers.

"First, 'I begin at the end.'," he said.

Tell me the Secret

"And this button," said Muirne. Mariota nodded.

"Second, 'I am nothing.'"

"And this pebble." Muirne held it up. Mariota smiled.

"Third, 'I am the moon.'" Dom waited for Muirne to show the berry.

"And this," she said at last. "But we think the fourth object is the stone itself and it also gives the answer."

"We don't know the exact words," Dom admitted and suddenly realised that was very important. Everything had to be accurate. The look on Muirne's face said she had realised that too. The stone itself, when its little holes were filled with the objects, was not the whole answer, would not be the final step towards breaking the spell.

"So what do you think the stone will say when you place the objects inside it?" asked Mariota. "It must be you who does that, Muirne, because you still have ownership of the stone." Muirne thought hard and Dom held his breath.

"It will say - 'I am complete.' - I think." Mariota smiled and both Dom and Muirne breathed freely again.

"Muirne, you must now place them there, but first I think you deserve to know everything. We have time, so relax. I have waited ten years for this, another few moments won't hurt."

Mariota looked longingly at the stone she had not seen for ten years.

"You are correct. It is a sacred stone and I was given it when I was born. My family, like yours, Muirne, have a long tradition of wise women in it. But the drui-ban who is specially chosen to roam between the Celtic worlds helping others, is given this. It was my habit since I was small to sit on that long stone within the sacred circle, the one removed by the monks, on mid-summer and mid-winter days. I always carried my little stone with me wherever I went. It has very special powers as you have both discovered."

"Muirne's singing enchanted Rochad," said Dom. "That was one of them, wasn't it?"

"Yes," said Mariota softly.

"Was the long stone meant to be in line with the others?" Dom waited, fascinated, for Mariota's reply.

"Yes. It had been there for time before memory. But my own little stone was stolen and the thief gave it to Muirne's mother for the new baby. It was a totally chance meeting. The thief is one of our people and could never use its powers herself. She handed it over to your mother for she had simply stolen it out of spite."

"The old lady was Deoca, wasn't she?" asked Muirne horrified.

"Yes. I cannot return to my people until it is freely given back to me by its new owner, you, Muirne. The tradition is that if the drui-ban does not have her stone for ten years, then she is condemned never to return home, belonging nowhere. Deoca has been waiting a long time for this day, the day when she will see me exiled forever."

"She's just wicked," said Dom, " no wonder she's a mate of Gorach's."

"Quite so, Dom. Deoca realised that your mother, Muirne, knew about me when your father carved my name on the stone. She thought your mother had discovered that if the stone was returned to me, I would be free. But your mother has never known that. Your mother only knew that someone called Mariota had always sat on that stone and that the small stone had also belonged to someone called

Mariota. It was a tale handed down through the wise women of your family. Your mother had an idea that the two Mariotas and the two stones were connected but she knows absolutely nothing else. It was just by chance that the long stone was found. But Deoca panicked and spirited your mother away to make doubly certain the stone would never be mine again. You are just a young girl, Muirne, and Deoca didn't think you would be capable of solving the puzzle if you ever learned of it. She did not see you as a threat at first."

"But can you rescue Mother, Mariota?" Mariota nodded.

"I will free your mother from her when I have my powers back. When my friend heard that your father had carved 'Mariota' instead of what the abbot had ordered him to do, he saw that as a sign that your parents were on our side and that Deoca could be defeated. He knew from me that you had been given the stone by Deoca and only you could break the spell and return the stone to me. He also realised that you could not achieve so much alone, so the black dog was summoned to fetch Dom. They're old friends," she added smiling.

"Is the monk I spoke to in the abbey your friend, Maritoa, the one who was writing behind the sacristy door?" asked Muirne. Mariota smiled.

"Yes. Your mother had been told by her grandmother that that stone had been my favourite resting-place. But she did not know about the spell I was now under. Returning the stone to me will set both your mother and me free. Muirne, your father has not been in any danger, in fact, he has not left Mull. He was merely summoned by the abbot to explain why he had rendered the stone useless. The abbot is visiting friends nearby. Your father had no need to go over to Iona. My friend should have told you that. I shall speak to him very sternly when next we meet."

"Don't be too hard on him, Mariota, for he was only trying to do his best for you. What has happened to the little bird," said Muirne.

"It's safe and sound. It really is his pet. It comes and goes as it pleases. Now, Muirne, once you place the three objects into the stone and then hand it to me, all will be as it always was. Your mother will be safe and it will be as if nothing has changed, nothing has happened. No-one will have any memory of her absence."

"Except the abbot will be still be mad about the stone," said Dom, practical as ever.

"Then perhaps Muirne's father can suggest to him that the stone should be kept at St Ernan's as it would be of no use on Iona. I think the abbot will not care very much where our stone finally comes to rest. We know it will be sacred wherever it is. Perhaps Muirne's father could create some beautiful plans for carvings for the cloister pillars that will pacify the abbot," suggested Mariota.

"Come on, Muirne, get on with it. The sun's about to set and I want to get home for my tea. I'm hungry."

"Patience, Dom," said Mariota and they watched as Muirne made the stone complete.

"Thank you both," whispered Mariota as Muirne handed the stone to her. "Never forget me for I will always be with you. Both of you. Remember that."

"Will you always be near the stone on mid-summer's day? And mid-winter's day?" asked Muirne hopefully.

"I told you," said Mariota softly, "nothing has changed."

Dom walked slowly back along the village street. The tourists had gone, Muirne and Mariota, too. Even the black dog had left and the sun finally slipped beneath the horizon.

chapter 18

Dom sat on the moss- covered, dry-stane dyke that separated the ruined church of St Ernan's from the lush green fields surrounding it. Cattle grazed in them contentedly for St Ernan's and the world about it seemed that kind of place. It was a place where nothing had ever happened but the age-old routine of the church and its people and the seasons. His eyes travelled beyond the little knot of people within its remaining walls, beyond its ancient, crumbling edifice and over the tall Celtic cross and memorials to past lives now mostly forgotten. They finally rested on the blue, silent waters of Loch Assapol. All was still in the drowsy sunlight of the late afternoon, the salmon and brown trout seemingly having better things to do than get hooked by fishermen.

Dom's fingers carefully unravelled the little scroll he had taken from his backpack. He smiled as the familiar plan reminded him of a wondrous story no-one would ever believe before he reluctantly replaced and zipped the pocket shut. A voice suddenly sliced through the soft, warm air.
"Who was she, do you think?"
"Mariota?" came the reply.

Tell me the Secret

"Yes." It had become a group discussion as they all chimed in.

"A Viking princess?"

"Not a Viking name."

"A prioress from the nunnery?"

"Related to a Scottish king?"

"A wife he was fed up with?

"Stuck her in the nunnery?"

"Which Scottish king was that?" The boys were now interested.

"Depends on when she died."

"Does it say?"

"No." The first voice now bellowed out again,

"Miss, who was this Mariota?" The supply teacher struggled with her notes, squinted at the grave-slab and then gave up. Maybe she would try varifocals. That might help, she thought. It had been a long, gruelling day and they were due back at the ferry.

"You're supposed to read the notes that have been placed there to give you all the relevant information. Anyway, whoever she was, she's dead." 'Miss' had run out of patience.

"No she isn't. I know her. I know Mariota. She's a friend of mine." A different voice this time, a confident one.

"Dom Broadley, if you've nothing sensible to say then say nothing."

"Nothing was what it was all about, Miss, in an odd sort of way," said Dom smiling, getting up from the low wall and joining the rest of the class. And she's definitely not dead, he said to himself, and neither is Muirne. Dom Broadley was content, for as long as the black dog came for him,

Dom knew that the pathway to their world would always be open to him.

Book 1 in the *Dom Broadley* series is *Don't Go There*.

Dom's emotions see-saw between fury at being wrenched from his home in Glasgow to sheer terror when accosted by these fierce people of the 14th century.

With his new ability to move between past and present with the help of the Black Dog, Dom is convinced his mind is about to blow. What if he is suddenly unable to return to the present? He learns he has just one week to prevent this battle to the death and free himself from the spell. Can he do it and still remain sane?

Printed in Great Britain
by Amazon